Curse
of the
Connecticut
Coyotes

Here's what readers from around the country are saying about Johnathan Rand's AMERICAN CHILLERS:

"I love your books! Everyone in my school races to get them at our library. Please keep writing!"

-*Jonathon M., age 13, Ohio*

"I am your biggest fan ever! I'm reading MISSISSIPPI MEG-ALODON and it's awesome."

-*Emilio S., Illinois*

"I just finished KENTUCKY KOMODO DRAGONS and it was the freakiest book EVER! You came to our school, and you were funny!"

-*Ryan W., age 10, Michigan*

"I just read OKLAHOMA OUTBREAK. It was really great! I can't wait to read more of your books!"

-*Bryce H., age 8, Wisconsin*

"My mom ordered American Chillers books on-line from your website, and they were autographed by you! Thanks!"

-*Kayla T., age 11, Louisiana*

"I love to read your books at night, in bed, under the covers with a flashlight! Your stories really creep me out!"

-*Chloe F., age 8, California*

"Man, how do you come up with your crazy ideas? I've read 15 American Chillers, and I don't know which one I like best. Johnathan Rand ROCKS!"

-*James Y., age 10, Nebraska*

"Ever since you came to my school, everyone has been addicted to your books! My teacher is reading one to us right now, and it's great!"

-Mark F., age 11, Kentucky

"You need to put more pictures of your dogs on your website. I think they're super cute."

-Michelle H., age 12, Oregon

"I have read every one of your American Chillers and Michigan Chillers books. The best one was WICKED VELOCIRAPTORS OF WEST VIRGINIA. That book gave me nightmares!"

-Erik M., age 9, Florida

"How do you come up with so many cool ideas for your books? You write some really freaky stuff, and that's good."

-Heather G., age 8, Maryland

"I met you at your store, Chillermania, last year. Thanks for signing my books for me! It was the best part of our vacation!"

-David L., age 13, Illinois

"A couple of years ago, I was too young to read your books and they scared me. Now, I love them! I read them every day!"

-Alex P., age 8, Minnesota

"I love your books, and I love to write. My dream is to come to AUTHOR QUEST when I'm old enough. My mom says I can, if I get accepted. I hope I can be a great writer, just like you!"

-Cynthia W., age 8, South Dakota

"Everyone loved it when you came to our school and did an assembly. You were really funny, and we learned a lot about writing and reading."

-Chad R., age 10, Arizona

"You are my favorite author in the whole world! I love every single one of your books!"

-Amy P., age 9, Michigan

"I heard that you wear those weird glasses when you write your books. Is that true? If it is, keep wearing them. Your books are cool!"

-Griffin W., age 12, Maine

"HAUNTING IN NEW HAMPSHIRE is the best ghost story ever! EVER!"

-Kaylee J., age 11, Tennessee

"I don't think anyone else in the world could write as good as you! My favorite book is NEBRASKA NIGHTCRAWL-ERS. Britney is just like me."

-Taylor, M., age 10, Michigan

"I used to hate to read, and now I love it, because of your books. They're really cool! When I read, I pretend that I'm the main character, and I always get freaked out."

-Jack C., age 9, Colorado

Got something cool to say about Johnathan Rand's books? Let us know, and we might publish it right here! Send your short blurb to:
Chiller Blurbs
281 Cool Blurbs Ave.
Topinabee, MI 49791

Other books by Johnathan Rand:

#28: Curse
of the
Connecticut
Coyotes

Johnathan Rand

An AudioCraft Publishing, Inc. book

American Chillers #28: Curse of the Connecticut Coyotes
ISBN 13-digit: 978-1-893699-74-8

Librarians/Media Specialists:
PCIP/MARC records available **free of charge** at
www.americanchillers.com

Cover illustration by Dwayne Harris
Cover layout and design by Sue Harring

Printed in USA

Dickinson Press Inc., Grand Rapids MI, USA • Job 3753200 July 2010

CURSE
OF THE
CONNECTICUT
COYOTES

1

"Hey, Mom," I called out from my bedroom. "Have you seen my hairbrush?"

I'd looked all over for it. Usually, it's on my dresser, but once in a while, I misplace it.

Like tonight.

"No, Erica, I haven't," Mom replied from the kitchen. "Did you check the bathroom?"

"Not yet," I said. Barefoot, I strode out of my bedroom, down the hall, and into the bathroom. I turned on the light and glanced around, but I didn't see any sign of my brush.

Where could it be? I wondered. I usually don't

take it out of my bedroom.

Odd.

I turned off the light, left the bathroom, and walked to the kitchen where Mom was busy pulling out pots and pans from a cabinet beneath the counter.

"It's not in the bathroom, either," I said.

"I don't know where it is," Mom replied. "Maybe gremlins stole it."

I rolled my eyes. Whenever something is missing in our house, Mom blames it on gremlins. Usually, it's Dad who loses things, and usually, it's his car keys or his wallet. He gets really frustrated and turns the house upside down trying to find whatever he's misplaced. And, of course, he usually finds the item right where he left it.

Things are always found in the last place you look, Mom always says.

Which makes a lot of sense. After all: once you find whatever it is you're looking for, you don't have to keep looking, because you've already found it . . . in the last place you look.

But I still had no clue where my hairbrush was, and I wanted to find it before I went to bed.

I stood in the kitchen, thinking, while Mom

scurried about. She was experimenting with some kind of new cake recipe. Pots and pans were stacked on the counter, and there were plastic bowls and utensils in the sink. She might have been making a cake, but she was also making a mess. She's a great cook, but she destroys the kitchen when she makes meals.

I looked out the kitchen window. The sun was setting, and the sky was orange and purple. It would be dark soon. My little brother, Cole, was playing in the yard. My mom always somehow managed to juggle pots and pans and keep an eye on him.

I watched Cole run past our picnic table and vanish. Cole is only three, and he's always getting into some sort of trouble, always making some kind of mischief. I'm eleven, so I'm a lot older . . . and I always seem to be bailing him out of trouble.

And he can be a pest, too.

Like now.

In the gloomy dusk, I saw something I recognized sitting on the picnic table.

My hairbrush.

"There it is!" I said to Mom as I pointed. "My brush is outside! What's it doing out there?"

"Maybe the gremlins left it there, Erica," Mom

replied, without looking up from the mixing bowl in front of her.

Yeah, right, I thought. *Gremlins, nothing. Cole took my brush. He took my brush and left it outside.*

I stormed across the kitchen and slid the glass door open.

"Cole!?!?" I shouted. My voice echoed through the neighborhood. "Where are you?!?!"

He didn't answer, but I could hear him at the far end of our backyard, where the grass ended and the forest began. With nightfall approaching, it was hard to see him. But he was talking to himself, which he does a lot.

I strode across the grass to the picnic table. The blades were cold and wet against my bare feet. I could smell the thick scent of a wood fire, and I figured someone on our block was having a cookout. That's just what it's like in Fairfield, Connecticut. Lots of people have cookouts, barbecues, games, get-togethers . . . especially in our neighborhood. All the neighbors know each other, and we have a lot of fun. I have a lot of friends on our block, and we never run out of things to do.

I was just about to pick up my hairbrush from

the picnic table when Cole's words in the darkness caught my attention.

"Nice doggie," he said. "Pretty, pretty doggie."

Alarmed, I stopped and turned, straining to see in the gloom.

"Cole?" I called out. "Is there a dog with you?" I was worried. Cole was too young to know that it was dangerous to pet unfamiliar dogs, too young to know that he should stay away from dogs running loose.

"Cole?" I said again, and I started walking toward his voice. "Is there a dog in the yard?"

As I drew closer, I could make out his white shirt, but it was still too dark to see anything else. He was only a ghostly form against a black curtain of night.

"Nice doggie," Cole said again. "Good doggie."

"Cole," I said, "You shouldn't—"

Suddenly, I saw the animal that Cole was speaking to, and I stopped calling to him.

I froze.

My blood chilled.

Oh, no! I thought. *That's not a dog! That's MUCH worse!*

2

It was a SKUNK!

I could see the white stripe on her back, and I could make out the shadowy form of her body. She wasn't very big, really—probably about the size of a normal cat—but that didn't matter. My little brother thought it was a dog!

"Cole Allen Falkner," I said sternly, "come here *right now*." Whenever I *really* need to get my little brother's attention, I use his full name. My mom does the same thing to me when she wants my attention.

"I wanna play with the doggie," Cole said.

"Cole, that's not a dog," I said, drawing in a nervous breath. "That's a *skunk*. And if you don't come here this very minute, she's going to spray you, and you're going to stink like a skunk."

"Huh-uh," Cole said. "I wanna play with the nice doggie."

I knew I had only a few seconds. It was just a matter of moments before the skunk would turn, raise her tail, and spray Cole. He'd stink for weeks! Not only that, he'd make our house stink. Everything in our home would smell like skunk . . . including *me*.

I decided to take a different approach. Instead of trying to make him come to me, I decided to be nice.

"Cole," I said sweetly, "if you come to the house right now, I'll get you a big bowl of chocolate ice cream. I'll even put a scoop of peanut butter on it, just how you like."

Cole paused. Then: "Really?" he asked.

"Really," I replied. "But you have to come here right now."

It worked. Cole turned and walked toward me, and the skunk waddled off into the darkness.

I let out a sigh of relief. Cole had no idea how close he'd come to being sprayed. I've often called my brother a 'little stinker,' but I only meant it as a joke. If that skunk would have sprayed him, he would have been a *real* little stinker!

"I love ice cream!" Cole said.

"I know you do," I replied. I took him by the hand, and we walked to the house together. "I'll get a big bowl, just for you."

"I can't find Teddy," Cole said.

"You lost your teddy bear?" I asked. Cole has a brown and white stuffed bear that he takes everywhere.

"Uh-huh," he replied.

"He'll turn up," I said. "Like Mom says: things are always found in the last place you look."

Inside our house, the mess in the kitchen had grown to monstrous proportions. There was flour and dough and cake mix all over the cupboards, the counter, and even on the floor. Mom, covered in flour herself, was busy looking at a recipe. She had a confused look on her face, like she was trying to figure something out. Like I said: Mom's a good cook, but when she makes something, she *destroys* the kitchen.

"Go get your pajamas on," I said to Cole, "and I'll get your ice cream."

"Goody!" Cole squealed, and he ran to his bedroom.

While he was gone, I explained to Mom about the skunk in the backyard and how close Cole had come to being sprayed.

"Your father said he saw a skunk last week," Mom said. "That's probably the same one. That was very good thinking on your part to keep your brother from getting sprayed."

I took the ice cream from the freezer, scooped out a blob, and put it in a bowl. Then, I got the peanut butter from the cupboard and plopped a big wad of it on top of the ice cream. Cole would be in heaven. It was his favorite treat in the whole world.

Then, I remembered my hairbrush. I'd left it on the picnic table.

"Be right back," I said to Mom. "I left my brush outside."

"Things are always found in the last place you look," Mom said.

I rolled my eyes, pulled the sliding glass door open, and slipped outside.

The sun had set, and there was only a faint, orange glow in the west, like lava in the sky, seeping away. The smell of wood smoke had faded, and the cool night air tickled my nostrils. The grass beneath my bare feet was cold, and my skin broke out in goose bumps. It wouldn't be long before winter came, and I would have to wear shoes or boots when I went outside.

I reached the picnic table, picked up my hairbrush, and was about to return to the house.

That's when I heard a noise.

It was just a rustling of leaves, very soft and quiet. The skunk was still around, I was sure, and I was once again glad that Cole hadn't been sprayed.

I peered into the dark backyard, looking for the creature, but it was too dark.

No matter. It was just a skunk. No big deal. You've seen one skunk, you've seen them all. I just didn't want to get too close to it.

The noise came again, louder this time. I heard a growl.

Weird, I thought. *Skunks don't growl.*

And then, I *did* see something.

Not a skunk.

Not even the shape of a skunk.

In fact, I had no idea exactly what I saw—not at the moment, anyway.

At the back of our yard, in the dark of the new night, were two glowing red sparks.

Eyes, burning like hot coins.

Staring.

At *me*.

Something horrible was in our backyard, watching me at that very moment!

3

Gripped by fear, I could only stare at the two sinister red eyes glaring back at me in the dark. I wanted to shout, to scream for help, but it felt like iron claws had wrapped themselves around my body, squeezing the air from my lungs. I couldn't even breathe.

What is that thing? I wondered. *And why are his eyes glowing?*

I'd never seen anything like it before. I was sure it was an animal of some sort . . . but what kind? It was too big to be a skunk, as the eyes were too large and too far off the ground. I wondered if it might be a dog, but I'd never seen a dog with glowing red eyes before.

Somehow, I found the courage to move. I took a step backward, then another, and another. At the far end of the yard, the red eyes remained where they were, motionless, boring into me like laser beams.

When I reached the sliding glass door, I pulled it open, darted inside, and slammed it closed. I let out a huge sigh of relief.

The noise from the slamming door caught Mom by surprise, and she looked up from her mess in the kitchen. There were several flour smears on her face and chin.

"Erica," she said sternly. "I've told you a thousand times not to slam the sliding glass door."

She must have noticed the terrified expression on my face, because her stern look vanished and was replaced with alarmed curiosity.

"What's wrong?" she asked.

"There's something freaky out there!" I replied. "Something with red eyes! I saw it! It's in the backyard, by the trees!"

Mom put down the mixing bowl she was

holding and hurried toward me. She flipped on the outside porch light and peered out the sliding glass window.

"I don't see anything," she said.

The porch light lit up the backyard, giving it a cool, lemony glow. The shadow cast by the picnic table looked like a hungry monster, stretching out over the grass to become one with the darkness.

But there was no sign of the glowing red eyes.

"I'm telling you," I insisted, "I *saw* something. There was *something* out there. I don't know what it was, but it had red eyes. It was watching me."

We stood at the sliding glass door, peering outside. We saw no glowing red eyes or any animals. Nothing moved.

"I'm sure it was probably just a dog," Mom said. "I hope he doesn't tangle with that skunk."

Mom was probably right. It probably *was* a dog. Still, we don't see many stray dogs around our neighborhood. Some of the people on our block have dogs, but they keep them in their own yards, and they don't run loose.

No matter. I was safe inside. Whatever I saw, it was *out there.* It couldn't get me. I had no reason to be afraid.

Not *yet,* anyway.

But soon.

Soon, I would find that I had good reason to be afraid . . . and it all started later that night, when I was awakened by something very, very strange . . . .

4

Later that night:

I awoke in bed with a book folded open on my chest. I'd fallen asleep reading. It was a book about a kid that was a wimp, and it was really good and very funny.

The light beside my bed was still on. I put the book on my nightstand, clicked off the light, and pulled the covers up to my chin. I closed my eyes and, after a few minutes, began to drift back to sleep.

A noise outside jolted me awake.

A squealing, laughing sound.

A howl.

I sat up in bed. The howl came again, and I knew what it was.

A coyote. Maybe a couple of them.

We hear them once in a while, usually late at night. Sometimes, we see them. Not very often, though. For the most part, coyotes hunt for food after dark, so it's not very often that we see them during the day.

The howl came again, closer this time. In fact, it sounded like it might be coming from our front yard or in the street.

I scrambled from my bed and tiptoed to the window. Outside, the streetlight gave off a salty blue glow, illuminating our yard and part of the neighborhood. I could see our neighbor's homes and cars parked in driveways. Dark shadows were splayed everywhere, frozen and motionless like jagged, black icebergs.

Something moved.

Just a small shadow, near a tree in our neighbor's yard. I watched for a moment, until it moved again.

Then, the animal strode out into the light. I was right! It *was* a coyote! It was about two feet tall, skinny, and long. I couldn't tell what color he was, because it was too dark, even in the glow of the streetlight. But most of the coyotes I see are a dirty, dark gray or brown.

While I watched, the animal sauntered across our front yard. He didn't appear to be in any hurry either, and I was sure that he wasn't afraid of anything. After all: he was a creature of the night. At night, this was his territory. While other animals slept, he was out hunting for food. Coyotes have a keen sense of smell, hearing, and vision that make them superior night hunters.

Suddenly, the animal stopped. He turned his head and looked directly at me. I hadn't made a move or done anything to draw his attention . . . but he saw me, I was sure. He was watching me. Just like—

And that's when his eyes began to glow red, just like the animal I'd seen in the backyard!

5

That's what I saw in the backyard earlier tonight! I thought. *He has the same glowing red eyes!*

I watched the creature watch me. He didn't come any closer; rather, he remained standing in the yard, his head low, staring.

At *me.*

How can an animal have eyes that glow? I wondered. It didn't seem possible. Yet, the coyote's eyes were bright red, glowing like flashlights. I've never heard of any animal being able to do that.

A movement across the street caught my attention, and I flinched. Another coyote appeared, strolling to meet up with the one in our yard. Now, both of them were staring at me. Both of them had the same bizarre, glowing red eyes.

In the distance, I heard another coyote howl. My window was closed, so I couldn't hear very well, but it was a howl, all right. The sound caught the attention of the two coyotes in the front yard. They looked away for a moment before returning their gaze to me.

This is just plain freaky, I thought, and I was glad I was inside. I'd never heard of coyotes bothering humans before, but something told me these weren't ordinary coyotes. There was something about these creatures that wasn't right, especially the way they glared at me with their glowing eyes.

The strange animals watched me for another few minutes. Then, as if responding to some unseen signal, both turned and walked away, slinking into the night, vanishing among the pools of shadows.

I remained at the window, watching, wondering if I would see them again. Wondering what they *really* were, where they came from. I decided to tell Mom and Dad about them in the morning. Maybe Dad would know why their eyes glowed. Maybe some coyotes have the ability to do that.

I climbed back into bed, closed my eyes, and fell asleep.

In the morning, I was awakened by the squawk of the television set. The volume was blaring. Cole is always the first one up at our house, and he goes straight into the living room, turns on the television, plants himself on the floor, and watches cartoons. He'd sit there and watch TV all day if he could, but Mom and Dad won't let him.

I climbed out of bed, stretched, and looked at myself in the mirror. My curly, blonde hair was tangled and messy, and my nightgown was wrinkled. I was glad my friends at school didn't see me like this!

I'd forgotten all about the strange episode the night before with the two coyotes and their glowing red eyes. In fact, I didn't even think about them again . . . until I walked into the kitchen. I had just reached into the cupboard and pulled out a box of corn flakes, when I glanced through the kitchen window and into the backyard. There, I saw something so horrifying that I dropped the cereal box. The top popped open, and corn flakes spilled out like crispy snow on the floor at my feet. I hardly noticed the mess I'd made.

Outside, in the backyard near the picnic table, was a dead cat.

It had been torn to shreds!

6

I stared in horror at the scene in the backyard.

The sun was coming up, and the grass was shiny with dew. The poor cat lay in a torn, battered heap. Sometime during the night it had been attacked by an animal . . . and I had a pretty good guess as to what that animal was.

I walked over to the sliding glass door. Corn flakes crunched beneath my feet, and some of them stuck to my skin. I didn't care.

My nose touched the sliding glass door. It was

cold, and my breath created a foggy cloud on the smooth surface.

Oh, for gosh sakes, I thought as I stared at the animal in our backyard. Then, I laughed out loud.

It wasn't a *cat* in the grass . . . it was Cole's teddy bear! I remembered him looking for it last night . . . and there it was, in the grass, not far from the picnic table.

I was relieved, but something bothered me. I was glad that it hadn't been a cat . . . but Cole's stuffed animal had been ripped apart by *something.* My brother would be heartbroken. He *loved* his teddy bear. Now, it was in shreds, torn apart, with puffy, white stuffing strewn all over the grass.

Did one of the coyotes do it? I wondered. *Why? Why would a coyote tear apart a harmless stuffed animal?*

I hurried back to my bedroom, dug my slippers out of my closet, put them on, and tiptoed into the kitchen. In the living room, my little brother was still mesmerized by the colorful images on the television, and I hoped to go outside and pick up Teddy (what was left of him, anyway), so Cole wouldn't see what had happened to him. Maybe I could use my allowance

36

money to buy him a new one.

In the kitchen, my slippers crunched on the spilled corn flakes. They were scattered over the white tile floor like tiny autumn leaves. Now, I had two messes to clean up: Teddy in the backyard and the spilled cereal in the kitchen. The day wasn't getting off to a good start.

But it was still early. There was still plenty of time for things to get better.

Yet, that's not what happened. Things didn't get better: they got worse—the moment I walked outside.

7

I unlocked the sliding glass door and pulled it open. However, when I stepped outside, the sleeve of my nightgown caught on a piece of metal trim around the door. I hadn't realized it, and the moment it caught, I heard a loud ripping sound.

I froze and looked at my arm. There was a long, jagged tear up the sleeve of my nightgown, with several loose strings trailing.

Great, I thought. *What's going to happen next?*

One good thing:

It was Sunday, so I didn't have to be in a rush to get ready for school. Oh, I like school and all that, but Sunday is my favorite day of the week. Usually, I meet up with friends, and we always find something fun to do. My best friend, Haleigh Siegel, lives across the street. Another good friend, Brent Harper, lives just down the block and around the corner. I was sure I'd see them sometime today.

My slippers whispered in the dewy grass as I strode across the lawn to the picnic table. In the grass, Cole's teddy bear was tattered and torn into several brown and beige pieces. Clumps of fluffy white stuffing were strewn about.

Those coyotes really chewed that thing apart, I thought as I bent down to pick up the pieces. I wadded what was left of the stuffed animal into a ball in my hand, so that Cole wouldn't see it when I walked inside.

I looked around. Cheery birds were chirping in the trees. The sun was glistening on glittering leaves, and the sky was a beautiful, ice blue. A few thin, white clouds drifted like smoke.

A perfect morning.

And yet, as I looked around and into the

40

backyards of our neighbors' homes, into the trees and forest that began at the back of our yard, I couldn't help but wonder:

Is one of those things watching me right now?

It was an eerie thought. I'd never before thought of coyotes as something to worry about.

And why were their eyes glowing? Could I have just imagined it?

No, I hadn't. I knew what I saw in the backyard last night. And I knew what I saw in the front yard, too, when I looked out my bedroom window: Coyotes . . . with glowing red eyes. Crazy, yes . . . but seeing is believing.

I returned to the house. Cole was still glued to the television, and he didn't even glance in my direction when I entered the kitchen. I tossed what was left of his teddy bear into the garbage can beneath the sink and got to work cleaning up the corn flakes. What a mess! The entire box had spilled. I wound up using a broom and a dustpan to clean up the brittle chips.

So much for cereal, I thought. I scoured the cupboard, searching for something else to eat, but the only thing left was oatmeal. Blech! I don't like oatmeal, so I settled for a banana and a bagel.

Then, I went to my bedroom and changed into jeans and a heavy sweatshirt. Later in the day, it might get warm . . . but in the morning, the air was chilly, and a sweatshirt would keep me warm.

I looked at the glowing blue letters of my alarm clock. It was 7:15, which was too early to call Haleigh or Brent. Mom and Dad were still sleeping, too.

I brushed my teeth and combed my hair, then went into the living room. Cole didn't even notice me, as he was too absorbed in watching cartoons.

So, I decided to go into the garage and get my skateboard. I'm really not very good at the sport, but it's fun. And besides: I was bored. I figured I could kill some time in the driveway, riding around . . . at least for a little while.

But, in the garage, I had a problem. Dad must have figured that I wouldn't be using my skateboard for the rest of the year, so he'd put it on the very top of a rack of shelves. The metal rack was like a giant, gray bookcase, filled with cans of paint, power tools, tool boxes, rags, lawn and garden equipment . . . all sorts of stuff.

And, at the very top, my skateboard was upside down, wheels in the air. There was no way I could reach it. There was a ladder in the garage, but it was hanging on the wall. It, too, was out of reach.

So, I decided to climb up the shelves to get my skateboard.

Now, I *know* my dad had told me once before not to climb the metal shelves. He saw me doing it once, last year, and got mad. He told me to get down, that it was dangerous. I did what I was told, but I thought it was silly. After all: what could possibly happen if I climbed a simple, metal rack of shelves?

With both hands, I grasped the shelf that was at eye level. Then, I placed my foot on the bottom shelf. I began pulling myself up, shelf by shelf, like I was climbing the rungs of a ladder. It took only a few seconds to reach the top, and I reached up with my right hand to grab my skateboard.

All too late, I realized I was in serious trouble. I'm not very big, but my weight on one of the uppermost shelves was enough to cause it to become unbalanced. The shelf came loose, and I could feel myself falling back.

There was nothing I could do. The entire unit leaned over, and my skateboard slid from the top shelf and hit my shoulder as it tumbled. Before I knew it, the metal rack fell, and I went with it. I glimpsed the ceiling just before I hit the floor.

Then, everything went black.

8

Gray fuzz.

That's the first thing I was aware of, the first thing I saw. There were no sounds—not that I noticed, anyway—and I felt like I was all alone, drifting in a puffy cloud, immersed in the twilight of a dream.

I was confused, disoriented, and my head ached. I had no idea where I was, how I got there, what had happened. For a few terrifying moments, I couldn't even remember my name.

Then, my memory began drifting back.

My name is Erica Falkner, and I live in Fairfield, Connecticut, with my mom and dad and my little brother, Cole.

But where am I?

Soon, my vision cleared, and I recognized my surroundings. I was in the garage, staring up at the white ceiling. The back of my head was throbbing. I sat up slowly.

In front of me, the shelving unit lay on the floor, along with a few other items: cans, rags, tools, and bottles of household cleaners. A coffee can containing screws, bolts, and nails had overturned, leaving the small objects scattered about on the cement floor.

I raised my hand and felt the back of my head with my fingers. There was a large lump there, and it throbbed even more when I touched it. I pulled my hand away and looked at my fingers.

No blood, I thought. *That's a relief. But I must have hit the floor pretty hard.*

I looked at the metal shelving unit on its side. I was lucky. I could have been hurt badly if I'd hit my head any harder than I had. As it was, I was probably going to have a lump and a headache for a couple of days. But, for the most part, I was going to be okay.

Now that the unit was empty, it wasn't very heavy, and I was easily able to push it upright and against the garage wall. Then, I picked up all of the items that had fallen off. Thankfully, no liquids had spilled, and nothing had been broken. When I was done, it looked like nothing had happened.

No need to tell Mom or Dad, I thought. *Dad warned me not to climb on the shelves, and now I know why. I won't be doing that again.*

Later that day, Haleigh came over. She seemed really nervous when I opened the front door.

"What's wrong?" I asked.

She shook her head as she stepped into our house. "Nothing," she replied, pulling at a lock of her brown hair.

"I know you better than that," I said, searching her eyes. "You look like something's wrong."

"You'll think I'm weird," she replied.

"I think you're weird, anyway," I said with a smile. I was trying to get her to lighten up, but it didn't work.

"No, really," she said nervously. "I saw something really freaky on the way over here."

"What?" I asked.

"A coyote," she replied.

As soon as she said the words, a thin sheet of ice glazed my entire body. I knew what she was going to say next.

"But this wasn't a normal coyote," Haleigh continued. "This one had—"

"—glowing red eyes," I interrupted.

Haleigh's eyes flew open wide. She stared at me. "You . . . you've seen it?"

"Not just one," I answered with a nod. "Two. Maybe more. I saw one in our backyard, and then I saw two in our front yard, just last night."

"I didn't know coyotes can do that with their eyes," Haleigh said. "He looked scary."

"Where did you see him?" I asked.

"Near our house, in the woods," Haleigh replied. "Just a few minutes ago. He stood near the woods, watching me with those glowing red eyes. It gave me the creeps."

"I wouldn't worry about it," I said. "I was freaked out when I saw them. But coyotes don't attack people."

"Yeah, you're right," Haleigh said. "But it was still freaky. I just hope I don't see him again."

"Me, too," I replied.

Haleigh hung out for a couple of hours. After she left, I went into my bedroom to read. Trouble was, I couldn't concentrate. All I could think about were those coyotes with red eyes.

Earlier in the day, I'd told Mom and Dad about what I'd seen in the front yard the night before. Both said that it was only a nightmare or just my imagination.

Just before I went to bed, I stood at my window, staring out into the yard. It was dark outside, but streetlights illuminated the block. My head was still sore from the fall I took earlier in the day, but it was feeling a little better.

Mom tapped on my door and came into my bedroom.

"You're still worried about those coyotes?" she asked with a smile.

I nodded, and Mom shook her head.

"It was probably just a trick of light," she said. "Animals can't make their eyes glow. And coyotes leave humans alone. Don't be frightened. Now, climb into bed, and get a good nights' sleep."

"Okay," I said. "Good night." Mom left and

closed the door behind her.

She was right, of course. Coyotes don't have glowing eyes, and they don't bother humans.

Still, I couldn't get over the feeling that there was something really wrong in our neighborhood. In my mind, I could still see the coyotes and their burning red eyes and the way they looked at me, like they wanted something.

Something was wrong, all right, but I didn't know exactly what it was—until later that night.

9

A dream.

It started out with me and Cole in the backyard. We were tossing a large, blue plastic ball back and forth. Not my favorite thing to do, but Cole loves to play catch, and it was fun just to watch him chase the ball.

The cool thing was, in my dream, we were able to float off the ground and fly around the yard. It was a lot of fun.

This is really awesome, I thought as I hovered

over a bush.

But then I realized something else.

I'm dreaming. This is just a dream. A cool dream, for sure. Usually, when you're dreaming, you don't know that you are. That's why some nightmares can be so frightening: because you think what is happening is real.

I wish Haleigh and Brent could see me now, floating above the yard!

Suddenly, Haleigh and Brent appeared! Of course, it was all in my dream, but I thought it was strange that they appeared the moment I thought about them. And in my dream, they, too, were able to float off the ground. The four of us played catch, tossing the ball high into the air where each one of us could fly up and catch it. It was a very fun dream.

Soon, Cole became bored. He got his tricycle from the garage and was pedaling around the yard. He was even able to fly into the air on his tricycle.

"This is great!" Brent said as he tossed the ball into the air. I leapt up and floated into the sky to catch it. Hovering above the treetops, I looked down and saw Cole, Brent, and Haleigh.

But I also saw something else.

Three coyotes with glowing red eyes, hiding in the bushes at the edge of the yard.

They were watching Cole.

But not for long.

Suddenly, all three coyotes lunged for my little brother. I tried to shout, but no sound came out. In seconds, the coyotes were nearly upon Cole, only a few feet away, eyes glowing, mouths snapping, long fangs exposed. I knew I was dreaming, but the sight was still very terrifying.

And that's when I awoke to the sound of my brother screaming in his bedroom!

10

Cole was shrieking like crazy, and his tormented cries echoed through our dark house. I could hear thundering feet pounding the floor. The entire house seemed to shake and tremble as Mom and Dad raced from their room and down the hall to Cole's room.

I sat up in bed, propped up on my elbows. My clock read just after three in the morning.

Mom and Dad had reached Cole's bedroom, and he'd finally stopped screaming. I could hear him sniffling and crying, and I wondered what was wrong.

The memory of my dream was still fresh: floating in the air with Brent and Haleigh, Cole on his tricycle . . . and the horrible coyotes with the glowing red eyes. They had attacked him—

—at the exact moment I had woken up! At the exact same moment Cole had woken up!

A slow feeling of dread snaked through my body.

No, I thought. *It's not possible. No way.*

Could it be?

Did Cole have the same nightmare that I had?

No. It couldn't happen.

Still, I wondered.

Had he?

I pulled the covers back, swung my feet to the floor, and stood. Quietly, I padded to my bedroom door and opened it a tiny bit. Although I couldn't see into Cole's room, I could hear talking.

"What was your dream about, honey?" Mom asked.

"Mean doggies," Cole sniffed.

I opened my mouth in a silent gasp. My skin tightened around my flesh and bones.

"Mean doggies chased me," Cole continued.

56

"Don't worry," Dad said. His voice was calm and soothing. "It was only a bad dream. You're okay."

I felt bad for Cole. He was only a little kid, and I'm sure the nightmare frightened him terribly. When I was his age, I had a dream about a monster that was chasing me through the woods. It scared me so badly that I stayed away from the forest for an entire year.

But what was most disturbing was the fact that Cole had the same dream I had. It seemed impossible, but stranger things have happened, I guess.

Well, not only have stranger things happened, but stranger things were *about* to happen . . . like the frantic phone call I received from Haleigh later that very morning.

11

Cole finally went back to sleep, and I did, too. My alarm woke me up at seven. The beeping is really annoying, like a loud, pulsating wasp. I slapped the clock twice, and the noise stopped.

Monday, I thought. *Another school week.*

The phone rang just as I climbed out of bed. It was unusual to hear it ring that early.

Who could be calling at this hour? I thought.

I heard Mom pick up the receiver in the kitchen, and, after a moment, she knocked on my door and pushed it open.

"Phone, Erica," Mom said. She handed the receiver to me. "It's Haleigh."

Haleigh? I wondered. *Why would she be calling at this hour?*

I took the phone and placed it to my ear. "Hello?"

"Erica, did you have a weird dream last night?" Haleigh asked.

Now, how would she know to ask that? I wondered.

"Why?" I asked.

"Because I want to know," Haleigh insisted. "I had a dream last night that was so real it woke me up."

There it was again: that gnawing feeling of dread. It was slithering up my spine, spreading through my body. There was something really, really strange going on.

"Yeah," I said. "I *did* have a weird dream."

"And your little brother was attacked by three of those tomato-eyed, ugly werewolves, wasn't he?"

I almost dropped the phone. A feeling of horror rocked my bones, and I shuddered.

"How did you—"

"Because I had the same dream!" Haleigh said. "And Brent was in your dream, too, wasn't he?"

"Yes," I said, in a voice that was barely a whisper. *"I had the same dream. We were floating in the air—"*

"—playing catch with a blue ball," Haleigh finished. "And Cole was riding around on his tricycle. I know! I was there! I'll bet if we ask Brent, he'll say that he had the very same dream!"

My mind was reeling. I'd never heard about people experiencing the very same dream at the very same time. How could it happen? What was going on? Did the mysterious coyotes with the glowing red eyes have anything to do with it?

At school that day, Haleigh and I caught up with Brent in the lunchroom. We were seated at a long table. Dozens of students buzzed around, carrying red trays with food and square, red and white milk containers. Across from me, Haleigh was explaining her dream, and we could tell by Brent's reaction that our suspicions were correct: he'd had the very same nightmare.

"That's totally freaky," Brent said as he shoveled a spoonful of green beans into his mouth with a plastic

61

fork. "How could the three of us have the same dream?"

"Four," I corrected. "Don't forget that Cole had the same dream, too. He woke up screaming bloody murder."

"That's just *weird*," said Haleigh as she shook her head. "I don't have any idea how it could happen."

But I *did*. I had an idea why it had happened. I wasn't sure about it, and I knew that I was probably wrong, but it was the only possible explanation. There was only one way to find out, and I was going to try it later that night, when I went to bed.

After I fell asleep.

I wasn't sure if it would even work, but I was going to try.

You see, in my dream, I had been playing catch with Cole, flying around in the air, weightless, having a great time. As soon as I had wished that Haleigh and Brent were with me, they appeared in my dream . . . just like that.

Is it possible I can control my dreams? I wondered. *Was I responsible for bringing Haleigh and Brent into my dream? If so, were they even dreaming at all . . . or was it, somehow, real? Was there some sort of*

reality that existed in a different world? Maybe Haleigh,
Brent, and Cole had no choice but to be there, because I
had willed them into my dream.

Into my world.

Did the mysterious coyotes have anything to do
with it?

The truth I was about to uncover was even more
horrifying than I could have ever imagined.

12

Darkness filled my room. The curtains were closed, and the only light came from the glowing digits of my alarm clock. Everything was still and quiet.

I'd been laying in bed for over an hour, but I couldn't get to sleep. My mind was too busy, too occupied and awake to drift off. All I could think about was the dream from the night before . . . and the dream I'd hoped to have that night—if I could ever fall asleep.

You see, I figured that if I was right, if I really

could control my dreams, I was going to try to pull Haleigh and Brent in again. I was going to try to contact them in my dream. I wasn't sure if it would work, but I was going to give it a try.

Of course, there was always the fact that I might not even *have* a dream. But maybe I would. If I did, I was going to try my experiment. I would have to fall asleep first, and so far, I wasn't having much luck. That always seems to happen: the harder you try to fall asleep, the more awake you seem to be.

Earlier in the day, in the school library, I looked for information about coyotes. I couldn't find anything anywhere about coyotes that were able to make their eyes glow red.

Then, I searched for books about dreams. I didn't find a lot, but what I *did* find didn't answer my questions. One thing I really wanted to know was if there had been any cases of people who had been able to control their dreams. I found nothing.

Still, I was determined to try. I didn't think my dreams had anything to do with the strange coyotes . . . but, then again, maybe they did.

I tossed and turned for a while longer. The last time I looked at the clock, it was nearly midnight.

If I don't get to sleep soon, I thought, *I'm going to be awfully tired in the morning and sleepy at school. If I nod off at my desk, I'm going to be in big trouble.*

I rolled onto my left side for a while, then onto my right side. Still unable to fall asleep, I rolled onto my back. Finally, after laying wide awake for some time, I propped myself up onto my elbows . . . and it was then that I saw the glowing red eyes, glaring at me from inside my closet.

13

I didn't dare move. I didn't flinch. I didn't move a single muscle.

He's in my closet! my mind screamed. *There's a coyote in my closet!*

Right then, I wanted to be anywhere else but in my bedroom. Never mind how the creature got there. I wanted out. Even being outside in the yard would be better than being in my bedroom!

Suddenly, in the blink of an eye, that's where I was: in our front yard, in my nightgown. The grass was cold and damp beneath my bare feet, and the night air was chilly.

What in the world? I thought . . . and then I realized what was going on.

I'm dreaming. I'm in the middle of a dream. I had thought I was awake, but I really wasn't. I'd fallen asleep, and I was having a dream. That's how I was able to get from my bedroom into the front yard.

I looked around. The neighborhood looked like it always did at night, with one odd exception: there was a murky, blue haze that hung in the air like smoke, making everything appear a little bit fuzzy.

Strange.

Okay, I thought, *time for my experiment.*

I knew I was only dreaming, but, in my dream, my eyes were open . . . so, I closed them.

"Haleigh," I whispered. *"Come here."*

I opened my eyes, shocked to find Haleigh standing right in front of me. Like me, she was wearing a nightgown, and her feet were bare.

"It worked!" I exclaimed.

"What worked?" she asked. She looked around, confused.

"I brought you into my dream," I replied. "I'm

having a dream, and now you're in it. All I had to do was close my eyes and think about you being here."

"That's handy," Haleigh said. "How about wishing for a million dollars?"

I thought about it for a moment. "All right," I said. "I'll try."

I closed my eyes and thought about a million dollars.

I opened my eyes. Nothing had changed.

"Well, that didn't work," I said.

But then, we saw headlights approaching on the street. It was a truck—an armored truck, actually—and it stopped at the curb in front of our house. While we watched, a man climbed out, walked to the back of the truck, opened two doors, and began pulling out large cloth bags and dropping them in a large heap. There were ten in all, piled on the grass near the curb. When he was finished, the man returned to the cab and drove off into the night.

"Wow!" Haleigh exclaimed. *"We're rich! You wished for a million dollars, and that guy just dropped it off for you!"*

I shook my head. "Too bad this is just a dream," I said. "But wait. See if you can do it, too. Wish for

71

something."

Haleigh closed her eyes tightly. After a moment, she opened them and looked around.

"What did you wish for?" I asked.

"A giant, butterscotch sundae with whipped topping and nuts," she said.

We looked around. I expected to see an ice cream truck arrive and drop off the giant sundae for Haleigh, but none came.

"Let me try," I said, but I didn't even have to close my eyes. The moment I wished it, a giant blob of ice cream, syrup, white whipped topping, and nuts fell from the dark sky . . . right on top of Haleigh! She didn't even look like a person anymore . . . just a huge blob of white and bronze goo. It was unexpected, but it was funny, too, and I couldn't help but laugh.

"Funny," Haleigh scolded. "Real funny." Then, she licked her lips and grinned. "Hey," she said. "This is pretty good!"

"Wait," I said, and I wished the sundae away. In a flash, the ice cream was gone, and Haleigh had returned to her normal self, standing in front of me in her nightgown. She examined her bare arms curiously. Not a drop of the gooey sundae remained.

"How did you learn to do this?" she asked. "If we're having a dream, how can you control it?"

"I don't know," I said, shaking my head. "It's really strange."

Then, I remembered the glowing red eyes in my closet. That's how the dream had started, and I'd wished myself out of my room.

Remembering the coyote, of course, was a mistake. Because as soon as I had the thought, a pair of glowing red eyes appeared on the other side of the street. Then, another, and another. In the misty blue fog of my dream, I could make out their silhouettes in the darkness.

Haleigh saw them, too.

"That's what I saw the other day!" she said. "Coyotes with red eyes!"

One of the coyotes began walking, very slowly, toward us. Under the glow of the streetlight, I could see him better. He stood a couple feet tall, and his hair was scruffy and matted. His head hung low, and his nose twitched as he sniffed the air. His mouth was open a little, and I could see his sharp fangs. All the while, his eyes glowed red.

"Kick him out of your dream!" Haleigh said. *"Get*

rid of him!"

In my mind, I wished the coyote away.

He kept coming.

I closed my eyes tightly.

Go away, I thought. *All coyotes in my dream, go away.*

I opened my eyes.

The coyote was still stalking toward us. He slowed for a moment to sniff the bags of money near the curb. Then, he looked up, let out a low, deep growl . . . and started running toward us!

14

Haleigh shrieked.

"Do something, Erica!" she screamed.

I closed my eyes tightly. *Go away!* My mind screamed. *Go away, right now!*

I opened my eyes, but the coyote was still racing toward us.

"It's not working!" I said. "I'm trying to make him disappear, but it's not working!"

I wished Haleigh out of my dream, and she vanished. Still, the coyote kept coming at me. He was only a few feet away when he leapt. His mouth opened, and his fangs were bared. I turned sideways, knowing that I couldn't get away, but not wanting the horrible creature to tear into my throat.

In the blink of an eye, I was in my bed again. My heart was racing, and I was sweating. The coyote was gone. At the last moment, just as the animal was about to tear into me, I'd woken up.

I leaned up in bed and rested on my elbows.

This is just too weird, I thought. I couldn't understand what was happening to me. It seemed there were some parts of my dream I could control, but other parts, I couldn't. It was great that I was able to wish for and receive a million dollars or a giant ice cream sundae, even if they were only in my dreams. But if I couldn't stop a coyote from attacking . . . .

And what would have happened if I hadn't woken up? I wondered.

Sure, it was just a dream, but it seemed so very scary and real.

I scanned the darkness of my bedroom, remembering the glowing eyes in my closet. I saw nothing. The eyes in my closet had been part of my dream.

I laid back in bed and stared up at the dark ceiling. I had so many questions about my dreams and my ability to control parts of them.

And the coyotes.

There was something going on that I couldn't quite grasp. Something bigger, something sinister that I just couldn't put my finger on.

But I was certain of one thing: the coyotes weren't normal. Real coyotes don't have glowing eyes, and they don't attack humans.

These *did.*

And as I closed my eyes and thought about my dream, I had no way of knowing what was really happening . . . or how bad things were going to get.

15

The first thing I did in the morning at school was find Haleigh to see if she'd had the same dream. She said she did, but she told me that she woke up just before the coyote attacked.

That was a relief. At least she wasn't injured.

"That's super freaky," Haleigh said. "I wonder how you can do that?"

I shook my head. "I don't know," I replied. "I have no idea."

After school, I walked home. In the living room,

Cole had planted himself in front of the television, under the spell of some colorful cartoon. I went into my bedroom to read and do my homework.

Later, after dinner, Mom asked me to help Cole clean his room. For a kid, he sure makes a mess. He never puts anything away, and there were toys scattered all over his floor and under his bed. But he helped out a lot, and soon, we had finished. I went back to my bedroom to continue reading my book. I'd read only a few pages when the phone rang.

"I'll get it," I said, sliding off my bed. I put my book down, walked into the kitchen, and picked up the phone. The caller ID displayed *Siegel, Bruce.* That's Haleigh's dad's name.

"Hey, Haleigh," I said as I held the phone to my ear.

"Erica!" Haleigh shouted into the phone. "I think I found out what's going on with the coyotes! Can you come over?" she asked. She sounded frantic.

I looked at the clock. It was six-thirty.

"Yeah," I said. "I'll be right over."

I told Mom I was going to Haleigh's, and I would probably be a couple of hours.

"Don't be late," she said. "It's a school night."

I wonder what she found, I thought as I closed the door to our house and bounded off the porch. It wasn't raining very hard, so there was no need to wear a raincoat or take an umbrella. The sky was light gray, the color of pearly granite.

I sprinted across the yard and stopped at the shiny, wet street, looking both ways to make sure no cars were coming. Cool mist chilled my exposed skin.

And that's when I saw him.

Several houses down, standing in the middle of the street, was a lone coyote. He was glaring at me with glowing red eyes. We stared at one another for several seconds. Neither one of us moved.

Slowly, he began walking toward me.

Stalking me.

His steps were precise, cautious. His red eyes were focused and intense.

I had to make a decision: run back to my house or across the street to Haleigh's. I thought I was a little closer to Haleigh's, so I made my decision and ran, lunging across the street with giant, long strides.

The coyote started loping toward me, faster and faster . . . and I realized all too late that there was no way I could outrun him.

16

I was halfway across the Siegel's yard when I realized I wasn't going to make it to their house. Maybe I should have turned and ran home instead of running across the street, but now it was too late to go back.

And the coyote was running *fast!* He was coming at me full speed, and he wasn't slowing down.

An idea came to me. I'm not sure how or why, and at first it seemed silly. But something told me to listen to the voice in my head, telling me to take command.

So, I stopped running and faced the coyote. He was only about thirty feet away and would be upon me in seconds. His head was low, and his mouth was open. His red eyes gleamed like molten lava. Although he stood only a couple feet tall, this clearly was an animal that was not afraid of anything.

I raised my arms and pressed my hands forward, as if I was pushing him away. I held them there.

Go away, I thought. I closed my eyes, concentrating deeply. *Go away now,* I repeated in my mind.

I opened my eyes, prepared to face the creature head on, waiting to be knocked to the ground, waiting for his teeth to sink in.

The coyote was gone!

I quickly scanned the yard and the street. I had closed my eyes for only a few seconds. There was no way the coyote could have run off in such a short time. He had simply disappeared.

Had it really been there in the first place? I wondered. *Or is my mind playing tricks on me?*

I looked around and saw no sign of the coyote anywhere. It was as if he had simply vanished or had never been there at all.

Is it all in my head? I wondered. *Is my mind simply playing tricks on me?*

I knew that the brain was capable of powerful things. Perhaps what was happening was only my imagination.

But Haleigh has seen the coyotes, too, I reminded myself. *Not only in dreams, but in real life. It can't be just my imagination.*

The light rain dampened my skin. Thunder rumbled in the distance.

I turned and walked across the lawn to Haleigh's house. I had almost reached the front porch when the unthinkable happened: claws dug into my ribs, and I was knocked forward as a coyote attacked from behind me!

17

The coyote didn't strike me very hard, but it caught me by such surprise that I tumbled to the wet grass. I quickly rolled to the side and prepared to use my feet to kick the animal away . . . and that's when I saw the puzzled look on Brent's face.

"You!" I said, more relieved than anything.

"Gee," Brent said. "All I did was sneak up behind you and grab your waist. I didn't expect you to freak out."

"I was already freaked out," I said, getting to my

feet. The knees of my jeans had softball-sized wet spots from where I'd landed in the grass.

I told Brent about the strange coyote with red eyes, how it had come after me, and how I had 'wished' it away with my mind. Brent listened, eyes wide.

"That's crazy," he said.

I nodded. "I know," I said. "But Haleigh called me and said she found out something about the coyotes."

"She called me, too," Brent said. "She wanted me to come over."

We bounded up the front porch steps and rang the doorbell. The Seigels have a little brown dog named Bingo, and we could hear him inside, yapping like a crazed toy.

"That bark is enough to drive you nuts," Brent said. "I don't think I could take two seconds of that, if this was my house."

The front door opened, and Haleigh appeared.

"Hey, guys!" she said. "Come in! You've got to see what I found out!"

We walked inside. Bingo scurried around our feet, still barking up a storm.

"Bingo, shhh!" Haleigh ordered, but the dog didn't pay any attention to her. She held the front door open. "Outside, Bingo!"

That did the trick. The tiny dog bounded past us and onto the porch. Haleigh closed the door.

"Come and check this out!" Haleigh said, and we followed her to her bedroom, where she explained what she'd discovered.

"I was at the library, doing some research for my geography paper. While I was there, I remembered the coyotes and their red eyes. I decided to go back through the local newspapers to see if there had been any reports of anyone seeing anything like it. I went back almost one hundred years."

"One hundred years!?!?" Brent said. "That must have taken you forever!"

Haleigh shook her head. "Actually," she said, "it took only a few minutes. There is a computer program at the library that searches keywords. All I had to do was type in the name of the newspaper. Then, I typed in the words 'coyote' and 'problem.' Look at what I found!"

On Haleigh's dresser was a small pile of papers. "I made copies of all the old articles," she said. "Look at this one."

Haleigh handed me the sheet. It was a copy of an old newspaper, dating back to the year 1917. I read the headline out loud.

"Woman accused of casting spells on neighbors," I said. I looked up at Haleigh. "What does this have to do with coyotes with red eyes?"

"Keep reading," Haleigh said.

I looked down at the paper. Brent looked over my shoulder, and we read the story together. Basically, it was about a woman who lived alone in the woods. There had been a series of accidents and bad weather, and some of the local townspeople accused the woman of being a witch and casting spells. She was a witch, they believed, because she was seen walking with two wild coyotes that appeared to be her pets. Plus, there had been some heavy rains that destroyed some local crops. Some people even came down with strange illnesses, and they blamed everything on the woman, saying that she was a witch. The woman insisted that she wasn't a witch, that she'd raised the coyotes from pups after their mother was shot by a hunter. She said she didn't cast any spells on the weather or on people. All she wanted was to be left alone.

But most people didn't believe her. Their minds had already been made up: she was a witch, and that's all there was to it.

I frowned. "I don't get it," I said, shaking my head. "What does that have to do with—"

"There's a lot more to it," Haleigh said. "The woman got mad, so she decided to play along. She told people that she really *was* a witch, and that if they didn't leave her alone, she was going to cast even more spells on the town."

"But if she wasn't really a witch," Brent said, "how could she cast spells?"

"Beats me," Haleigh said with a shrug. "But things get even more interesting. Here." Haleigh picked up another paper with a newspaper clipping printed on it. "Read this one."

I took the paper. Brent, still looking over my shoulder, read the headline out loud.

"Strange dreams haunt townspeople," he said.

A chill went down my spine. I knew all about strange dreams, that was for sure.

Silently, Brent and I read the news story. Apparently, many residents reported having strange dreams about coyotes. Not only that, but some even said that, while they were awake, they saw the coyotes that had been in their dreams. They knew they were the same coyotes, because they all had glowing red eyes!

"I'll bet those are the same coyotes that are appearing around here!" said Brent.

"This is scary!" I said.

"You don't know what scary is," Haleigh said. "Now, read *this*." She handed me yet another news clipping. What I read wasn't just *scary*—it was terrifying in ways I had never imagined.

18

"This can't be true," Brent said as he finished reading the story. "It's not possible."

The story was about how the woman had vanished. She disappeared without a trace, but she had left a note nailed to the front door of her house, saying that she'd placed a curse on the town. She claimed in her note that sometime in the future, a strange breed of vicious coyotes would invade the town. People would be forced to flee, just to be safe. The woman did this, she wrote, to get back at the townspeople for being unkind to her. In particular, she was mad at the newspaper reporter, who was the person responsible for spreading the rumor that she was a witch.

And the woman also had written something else. In her note, she told the people of the town that they would see her in their nightmares. Shortly after she vanished, people began having terrible dreams about the woman and the coyotes with the glowing red eyes. There were even reports of people being attacked by the strange animals.

"But she wasn't a witch," I said. "She said so herself."

"Maybe not," Haleigh said, "but for whatever reason, her spell must have worked. It's not very smart to play around with spells and things like that. You don't know what you're messing with. Besides: the people believed she was a witch. Imagine how scared everyone must have been when they found her note!"

"So, what does it all mean?" I asked.

"For whatever reason," Haleigh said, "the spell worked, and it's still working. That's why we're seeing those creepy coyotes."

"But they might not even be real," I said, and I explained to her about the coyote that I'd seen just minutes before and how I'd sort of 'wished' it away.

"Well," Brent said, "if all we have to do is wish them away, we won't have any trouble."

"True," I said. "But it's still a little scary. Those things are the freakiest animals I've ever seen."

"It's almost like they're imaginary," Haleigh said. "Except, they're from the woman's imagination, from long ago."

The more I thought about it, the more it didn't make sense. An old curse? Imaginary coyotes with red eyes? What did it all mean? Why was all of this happening? I had no answers.

But the thought of strange coyotes with red eyes terrorizing our neighborhood really made me worry.

I looked out the window. The drizzle had stopped, and rain was dripping from tree branches and leaves. Bingo was in the yard, sniffing the trunk of a birch tree.

And at the far corner of the yard, two coyotes with blazing red eyes stood beneath a tree.

A cloudburst of horror swept over me. *"Look!"* I said, pointing. Haleigh and Brent both turned and looked out the window . . . just as both coyotes started running toward Bingo!

19

"No!" Haleigh shouted. She ran to the window and threw it open. *"Bingo! Run!"*

The little dog looked up at Haleigh and wagged his tail. He had no idea that there were two coyotes attacking, and he made no move to run from them.

"Wait!" I said. "Remember: they're not real. We can wish them away!"

"I'm wishing, but it's not working!" Haleigh said.

I remembered how I'd made the coyote in the

front yard vanish. I closed my eyes and made a pushing motion with my arms.

"Go away," I whispered. *"You're not real. Go away."*

When I opened my eyes, Brent and Haleigh were looking at me. They turned and looked out the window, then back at me.

In the yard, the coyotes were gone. Bingo continued to sniff the trunk of the birch tree. He had no idea of the danger he'd been in.

"Erica," Haleigh breathed. "How did you do that?"

I shook my head. "I don't know," I said.

"I tried to wish those things away, but it didn't work," Haleigh said.

"Me, too," Brent said.

"Maybe you're the only one who can wish them away," said Haleigh. She and Brent were looking at me like I was a weird animal. Actually, I *felt* weird, like I was different from anyone else. Like I had some sort of magical power that no one else had.

But maybe I did. After all, when Haleigh and Brent tried to wish away the coyote, it hadn't worked. Maybe, for some strange reason, I was the only one with that ability.

Freaky.

"Okay," I said. "Here's what we're going to do. We're going to go to the library and look for more information about that woman and the coyotes. I have a feeling that there's more going on than we know about. Maybe those coyotes are more than just imaginary."

"You think they might actually hurt people?" asked Haleigh.

I shook my head. "I don't know," I said. "I'm just saying we should try to find out more. If they are dangerous, maybe there is a way to stop them from appearing."

"I have a really bad feeling about this whole thing," Brent said.

We all did. What was going on was really, really strange. It was like having a jigsaw puzzle with a bunch of pieces missing. It was crazy to think that the coyotes might not even be alive, like real animals.

One thing was certain, however: things were about to get a lot weirder . . . and fast.

20

The library was only a few blocks away, but we were nervous as we strode along the sidewalk. Our eyes kept darting all around, looking for any sign of the strange coyotes. The sky was dark and gray. A few cold sprinkles of rain fell.

"I wonder what happened to that woman, all those years ago," Brent said.

"Maybe she got tired of people calling her a witch, and she moved away," Haleigh said. "I wouldn't like it if everyone in town treated me that way."

"I don't believe in spells and things like that," I said. "There has to be some other explanation."

"How do you explain animals that have glowing red eyes?" Haleigh asked. "I mean . . . animals just can't do that. I've heard of some fish doing things like that—"

"—and fireflies," Brent interjected.

"Right," Haleigh continued. "But I've never heard of animals being able to create light like that."

Up ahead, something moved in the bushes near a house. Startled, we stopped walking.

"What was that?" Brent whispered.

A branch moved.

We froze.

Suddenly, a red-winged blackbird exploded from the bush and flew off, and the three of us heaved sighs of relief.

"Glad it wasn't one of those coyotes," I said.

"Even if it was," Haleigh said, "you could have just wished him away, like you did before."

"But what happens if it doesn't work?" I said. "I don't know enough about what is going on or why. None of us do. The only thing we know is something about a strange lady and her curse, or whatever it is she did, all those years ago."

We rounded the block and saw the library in the distance.

But we also saw something else. The three of us stopped suddenly and stood motionless on the sidewalk.

Ahead of us, a block away, a woman was coming toward us.

A woman . . . walking with two coyotes!

21

I grabbed Haleigh's arm and held tight, and the three of us stood and stared. The woman and the two animals continued walking toward us.

"Oh, for crying out loud," Brent said. "It's only Mrs. Williams and her two dogs."

Brent was right. Now that the woman was closer, we could see that the two animals weren't coyotes, but dogs. Collies, in fact, that were about the same size as coyotes, but with a bit longer fur. Mrs. Williams, who lives on the other side of the block, was taking them for a walk.

I breathed a sigh of relief and let go of Haleigh's arm.

"I think we're all just a little freaked," Haleigh said as we started walking again. We waved and said 'hello' as we passed Mrs. Williams and her dogs. She nodded and waved back.

The library wasn't very busy, which was odd. Usually, there are lots of people milling about, seated at desks, tapping away at computers, and browsing the bookshelves. Haleigh took us to the computer she'd used to research information about the coyotes and the woman.

The trouble was, we couldn't find much more information. We searched through old newspapers on the computer for over an hour, through years and years of stories, and we found only the same articles Haleigh had found. We found a few short news stories about people seeing strange coyotes, but that was all.

"Rats," Haleigh said. "I was really hoping we'd find more information about those things."

"About what things?" a new voice asked.

We turned to see Miss Levine, one of the assistant librarians. Miss Levine is tall, with long black hair that she wears in a ponytail.

"Oh, just some weird animals," I said.

"What kind of weird animals?" she asked.

"Coyotes," Brent said.

"Yeah," Haleigh said. "Coyotes with glowing red eyes."

Miss Levine smiled. "Oh," she said. "You've heard about the curse, too."

Haleigh's jaw fell. "You've heard about it?" she asked.

Miss Levine rolled her eyes and smiled. "Who hasn't?" she replied. "I heard about the woman and her curse when I was a little girl. We used to scare ourselves silly with stories of coyotes with glowing eyes."

Brent spoke. "Did you ever see any?"

Miss Levine frowned. "Coyotes with glowing red eyes?" She laughed and shook her head. "No, it's only a story from long ago."

"We read about it in old news clippings," I said.

"Well, you can't believe everything you read, I'm afraid," Miss Levine said. "We used to read the stories, and we even made up our own. It was especially fun to go to her old house to tell stories about the wicked witch and her curse."

I looked at Haleigh, then at Brent. I knew what they were thinking.

"You mean, her house is around here?" Haleigh asked.

"Yes," Miss Levine said. "It's in the woods on the other side of the park. Do you know where the big oak tree is?"

We nodded. The tree she was talking about was an enormous oak, and it towered over the far side of the park behind the playground.

Miss Levine continued. "In the forest on the other side of the tree, there used to be a trail that led right to her house, but I think it's overgrown now. Not many people go there anymore. Most have forgotten about the woman and her curse."

"Does anyone live there anymore?" I asked.

Miss Levine shook her head. "No," she said. "After the woman moved out, no one wanted to live in her house. Nobody wanted to live in a house where a witch used to live."

I glanced at Haleigh, and I knew exactly what she was thinking. After Miss Levine had walked away, Brent looked at Haleigh and shook his head.

"Huh-uh, no way," he said. "We're not going to that creepy witch's house."

"She wasn't creepy, and she wasn't a witch," Haleigh said. "She only left town because people were bugging her. It would be cool to see her house!"

I agreed with Haleigh: it might be fun to see the old home where the woman used to live. But I was concerned about one thing.

"What if we see any of those coyotes?" I asked.

"Can't you just wish them away?" Haleigh asked.

I shrugged. "I can always try," I said.

"See?" Haleigh said to Brent. "There's nothing to worry about."

Oh, there was plenty to worry about, all right. Soon, we'd realize we were in trouble way over our heads.

22

Something wasn't right.

We'd walked through the park, which was only a few blocks from the library. Several young children were playing on the swing set, hanging from monkey bars and dipping up and down on teeter totters. A couple of adults stood nearby, talking and smiling. Towering above was the majestic oak, growing near the forest, just like Miss Levine had said.

And, just like Miss Levine had said, the trail must have been overgrown with shrubs and small trees. We couldn't find any sign of it.

"Let's just make our own trail," Haleigh said.

"What if we get lost?" Brent asked.

Haleigh rolled her eyes. "How in the world are we going to get lost?" she asked. "There are houses and streets everywhere. The forest isn't that big."

Haleigh reached out, pushed some branches aside, and trudged into the woods. Brent and I followed . . . and that's when I realized that something wasn't right.

"Wait," I said. Haleigh stopped and turned around.

"What?" she asked.

"I don't know," I said. "Something just feels kind of . . . *weird.*"

We looked around. The forest seemed darker than it should at that time of the evening. Quieter, too. In the park, I'd noticed birds chirping in the trees and crickets chiming. Here, in the forest, there were no sounds at all. We couldn't even hear the children playing in the park.

"It just doesn't feel right," I continued.

"Erica's right," Brent said as his eyes scanned the forest. "Maybe this isn't a good idea."

"You guys are the biggest chickens in the world," Haleigh said. "You heard Miss Levine. She said the whole story about the coyotes and the curse is made up."

"You're forgetting one thing," I said. "Maybe the story is made up, but you and I both know we saw those coyotes. And however strange it seems, I was able to pull you into my dreams. Whatever is going on, it's not normal. In fact, one of those creepy coyotes could be watching us right now, and we wouldn't even know it."

We continued looking around. Haleigh tried not to show it, but I could tell she was a little nervous.

"We'll be fine," she said. "It's just a house, right? An old house where nobody lives anymore. It's empty. Let's go find it."

Of course, Miss Levine didn't know it, nor did we . . . but the woman's old home wasn't empty. We were about to discover that there really *was* something living inside . . . and it wasn't human.

23

We made our way through the forest. I couldn't help but notice that with every step we took, our surroundings seemed to become darker and darker, like time was speeding up, and night was approaching. I thought it was just my imagination, but Brent noticed it, too.

"How come it's getting so dark?" he asked.

"It's because the witch put a curse on these woods," Haleigh said with a smirk. "Soon, it's going to be pitch black, and we'll be lost forever."

I could tell she was only joking, but something told me there might be a bit of truth in what she said. There *did* seem to be something very dark and sinister about the forest, which seemed to be pressing in on us with every step we took. It was eerie. It was as if the forest itself was alive, like it was some sort of creature that was watching us, perhaps even luring us into a dangerous trap. My mind began to wander, and I imagined the tree branches coming alive, swarming us like venomous snakes, coiling around us like wires, binding us together and holding us as prisoners.

We'd walked only a short distance when we discovered the old home. It was small, much smaller than my house, and it sat in the middle of a field overgrown with tall, wispy grass, shrubs, and saplings. Most of the windows had been broken out, and the roof sagged. Wood shutters, some half open, were gray and weathered. We stopped at the edge of the field and stared.

"Miss Levine wasn't kidding," Brent said. "No one has lived here in years."

"I wouldn't live here if you paid me," I said. "This place is falling apart."

"I never even knew this house was here,"

Haleigh said.

I shook my head. "Me neither," I replied.

"Do you really think this is the place where the witch lived?" asked Brent.

"She wasn't a witch," Haleigh said. "Remember? The people in town thought she was, but she said she wasn't."

"But what about the curse?" I asked. "How else can you explain the coyotes with the glowing red eyes?"

Haleigh shrugged. "Beats me," she said as she looked around. "But there doesn't seem to be any around here."

And that's when we heard a noise.

It wasn't the sound of branches snapping or the sound of a coyote howling.

It was a creaking sound.

Like . . . a door.

Out of the corner of my eye, I saw something move by the house.

"Look!" Brent hissed. He pointed at the old home.

The front door was opening . . . *all by itself!*

24

Time seemed to stand still.

The old door slowly creaked open, as if some invisible hand was pulling it. The sound it made seemed to scratch my skin, and I could feel every hair on my body standing up.

"Who's doing that?!?!" Brent hissed.

"It's probably just the wind," Haleigh whispered, but she didn't sound so sure of herself.

"There's not enough wind to do that," I said quietly.

The door was now completely open, but all we could see inside was darkness. Although the home sat in the middle of the field, tall trees blocked much of the sunlight, and the entire old house was cast in a strange, unearthly gloom.

"It's like it's waiting for us," Haleigh said. "Like it's alive or something."

"Houses aren't alive," Brent said.

Brent was right, of course. But I remember reading a book about a madhouse in Missouri. In the book, it was as if the house was alive, in its own weird way.

But this was different. I had a bad feeling about the house, the woman, her coyotes, and her curse. There was something going on that was far more serious than I had thought.

And more dangerous, I was sure.

Haleigh took a cautious step forward.

"What are you doing?" I asked.

"I just want to take a closer look," she said. "I want to see what's inside."

"I'm not going in there," Brent said, shaking his head.

"I'm not, either," Haleigh said. "I'm just going to

look through the doorway. I want to see what the inside of her house looks like."

I must admit: Haleigh was braver than I was. Here we were, in the middle of the woods, near a creepy old home . . . and the front door had opened all by itself.

Things don't get any creepier than that, I thought.

But I was about to be proved wrong.

25

Haleigh took another step toward the creepy old home. A gentle wind stirred some of the dead, brown leaves on the ground, and they skittered in little tornado circles, spinning madly. Bony tree limbs wavered and whistled in the breeze, and it seemed like they were speaking to us.

Stay away, the branches were saying. *Stay away from the house. Stay away . . . .*

Haleigh seemed to sense this, too. She stopped walking, but only for a moment to look up and around at all of the trees. Then, she looked at us.

"Come on, you guys," she said, taking another step. "It's only a house."

"Yeah," Brent said. "A house where the front door opens all by itself."

The more I thought about it, the more I realized that Haleigh was right: it *was* just a house. Sure, the front door *seemed* to have opened on its own, but there must be some reasonable explanation for it. Maybe the wind blew it open and closed all the time. Maybe someone at some time had kicked the door open, and now, every breeze that came along caused it to sway back and forth.

Whatever the reason, I told myself, *doors don't open by themselves. And there are no such things as ghosts.*

I stepped past Brent.

"Where are you going?" he asked.

"I'm going with Haleigh," I said, trying to sound brave. I was still a little nervous, but I didn't want Brent to know it.

"Oh, all right," he said, and he began walking. "But just for the record: I don't think this is a smart idea."

"You're just a scaredy-cat," Haleigh said.

The three of us walked through the grass, side by side, toward the old house. Our steps were slow and deliberate, and our eyes remained focused on the open door. From where we were, the only thing we could make out inside were dim shadows.

"I am *not* a scaredy-cat," Brent said. "I just don't think this is a good idea."

"You're just afraid that the witch is waiting for you in the house," Haleigh teased. "You think she's going to cast a spell on you."

"I'm not afraid of any old witch," Brent said. "Besides: the woman wasn't a witch. She was just an ordinary woman."

"How do *you* know?" Haleigh asked. "Maybe she *told* everyone she wasn't a witch, just to fool them. That would explain the curse."

The wind blew stronger, and the trees hissed.

Go back, the branches seemed to say. *Go back now. This is your last chance. Go back. Go back. Go—*

The door creaked again, opening a bit more. A dead leaf landed in my hair, and I pulled it away and held it in my hand, never looking at it. It felt dry and brittle, and I crushed it in my palm. The tiny fragments scattered to the ground.

"I think I just saw something move in the house," Haleigh said.

We stopped walking and stared through the dark, open doorway.

"Like what?" I asked.

Haleigh shook her head. "I'm not sure," she replied.

"Look who's the scaredy-cat now," Brent snickered.

Haleigh turned. "Oh, yeah?" she said. "I'll show you. I'm not afraid of some old house, and I'm not afraid of an old curse or coyotes with red eyes."

And with that, she stormed off . . . right toward the open door of the old home.

For a moment, I was tempted to follow after her. I wanted to be brave, to show Brent that I wasn't afraid . . . but I was. I *was* scared, and I was beginning to think that Brent *was* right: this wasn't a good idea at all.

Haleigh slowed as she reached the front door.

She stopped.

Leaned forward.

Peered inside.

Then, she turned toward us with a smile.

"It's empty," she said. "There's nothing in here at all."

She was looking at us, grinning . . . and never saw the horrible beast that came at her with lightning speed from inside the house.

26

The attack happened so fast that my brain didn't have a chance to process it. Before I could have done anything, the animal had already charged, Haleigh had leapt out of the way, and the vicious creature sped past her.

One second later, after I realized what had just happened, I burst out laughing. The 'horrible beast' was only a big, old opossum, and it must have been living in the old house. When Haleigh approached, it had been frightened, and it bolted past her, out the front door, and vanished into the forest.

Brent, too, began to laugh. After a moment, even Haleigh started laughing. She had been scared by the frightened animal, but when she realized it was only an opossum, she thought it was funny and laughed at herself.

"Man, that thing scared the hair off my arms!" Haleigh said as she looked at us.

"Me, too!" I said with a laugh. "I thought it was one of those creepy coyotes!"

"I'm sure glad it wasn't," Haleigh said. She turned and peered through the open door and into the darkened home. I half expected another opossum or some other animal to come barreling out, but none did.

Haleigh took a step toward the house. If she took just one more step, she would be through the front door.

It's strange how my emotions changed. As Haleigh took that single step into the old house, nothing was funny. Not the opossum or the fact that it had scared her. In fact, I was nervous and worried for Haleigh. Sure, she was being brave—

But what might be lurking in the old house? I

wondered. Miss Levine had said that no one had been living there for years and years. But what if she was wrong? What if there *was* someone there?

Or—

Some *thing?*

I decided I wasn't going to let Haleigh go into the house alone. I'd always heard the saying that there was safety in numbers, and I figured two people going into the old home would be a lot safer than one. Brent must have thought the same thing, because as I began walking, he followed. Maybe he was being brave, or maybe he was scared to be left alone. No matter. I felt better knowing that the three of us were in this together. We could be there for each other, if something went wrong.

Haleigh saw us coming and waited in the doorway.

"What do you see?" I asked as I approached.

She shook her head. "Nothing but monster opossum tracks," she said.

"If there's another one in there," Brent said, "I think I'm going to jump out of my skin."

"Let's hope if there is anything in there, it isn't one of those freaky coyotes with glowing eyes," I said.

"I don't know," Haleigh said, craning her neck to look inside the old home. "It looks empty."

Now that the three of us were together, we stepped through the doorway and into the house. Haleigh was on my left, and Brent was on my right. The three of us were like a tight knot as we entered the house and stopped.

We were in a small living room. There was no furniture, nothing on the walls. Dust and dirt covered the wood floor, and there were small animal tracks crisscrossing all over the place. I figured that the tracks belonged to the opossum or any of the other animals that had probably inhabited the abandoned house over the decades.

Above, the ceiling was constructed of long logs and planks. They were sagging and water stained, discolored by years and years of neglect. To our left, in the corner, was an old, decaying, black iron stove that was rusting away. The stove pipe that should have extended up to the ceiling had fallen, and it lay in jagged, broken pieces on the floor, like a black metal snake.

"I think Miss Levine is right," I said quietly. "I don't think anyone's been here in years."

On the far side of the room was a doorway, which led, I presumed, to a bedroom. It was the only other room in the house. I found it odd that there was no bathroom in the house, but, then again, years ago, people didn't have the modern conveniences that we have today. Years ago, people used outhouses. I quivered at the thought of having to go outside in the middle of winter if I needed to use the bathroom.

"Not much to see here," Brent said.

Haleigh pointed. "Let's see if there's anything in that room," she said.

"It's probably empty," Brent said.

Oh, it was empty, all right, but in that room, we were about to discover that we weren't in just a *little* trouble . . . we were in trouble with a capital 'T.'

27

The three of us slowly made our way across the small living room. I looked down and back and saw the tracks that our feet were leaving in the dirt and dust.

If there was this much grime on my bedroom floor, I thought, *Mom would ground me until the next century.*

"Be on the lookout for more of those opossums," Haleigh said. "There might be a whole family of them living in here."

Brent snickered. "That was pretty funny when

he scared you," he said.

"It's funny *now,*" Haleigh said. "It wasn't funny then. I thought it was one of those coyote-things."

"Let's hope we don't see one of those," I said.

"Let's hope we find out what's going on," Haleigh said.

We stopped when we reached the bedroom. The door was open partway, and when Haleigh pushed it, it gave out a loud, tired groan. It was obvious it hadn't been moved in years. The sound was so loud and remorseful that I thought the door was going to break off its hinges and crash to the floor.

Instead, it shuddered slowly open, exposing yet another floor covered by a thick layer of gray-brown dust and dirt. There was a window on the far wall that was cracked, but the glass was intact. Like the floor, it had a layer of film on it: so much that the trees outside looked fuzzy and out of focus.

And there were footprints on the floor, but they looked very different from the opossum tracks in the living room. In fact, the footprints in the bedroom looked more like—

Coyote tracks, I thought.

Also—

136

Footprints.

Human footprints, about the size of my own feet, or those of a—

Woman.

Brent and Haleigh saw the strange tracks at the same time I did.

"O . . . O . . . Okay," Brent stammered quietly. "Is anyone else getting the creeps?"

"I am," Haleigh said.

"I am, too," I said.

"It feels like something's in this room, watching us, right now," said Haleigh. "Can you feel it?"

"Yeah," Brent said.

"Me, too," Haleigh said. "Let's get out of here."

"Wait," I whispered. *"I just heard something."*

We stood in the room. I hadn't noticed it before, but Brent had grasped my hand. His grip was so tight that my hand hurt.

"What did you hear?" Haleigh asked quietly.

I paused for a moment, then spoke. "I'm not sure," I said. My eyes scanned the room, but my head remained motionless. "Maybe it was nothing. But I was sure that it sounded like—"

Laughter.

A *woman's* laughter.

At first, it was faint and distant and difficult to make out. As we listened, however, it became louder and clearer. It was definitely the sound of a woman laughing.

Then:

Another sound.

Howling.

"Those are coyotes," I said. "I've heard them before. I know what they sound like."

By now, the three of us were totally freaked. Brent still had a vicelike grip on my hand. If he squeezed any tighter, he was going to break every single bone below my wrist.

The sounds seemed to be coming from all around us, but we couldn't see anything. The woman's laughter seemed to be circling us, moving closer with every passing second. The coyotes were yipping and yapping, and they, too, seemed to be moving closer, circling all around us . . . but we saw nothing.

"Where are they?!?!" Haleigh shrieked. *"I can't see them!"*

"They sound like they're just outside the house," Brent said. "I'll bet—"

Brent was cut off by the slamming of the front door. Not only that, the old shutters on the outside windows suddenly slammed shut. The house was dark and gloomy, and the only light came from the slants in the wood shutters.

That was all just too much, and we wanted out. The three of us raced to the front door.

"It's locked!" I said as I tried to turn the knob. "It won't open!"

Haleigh ran to one of the windows. The glass had long been broken out, and she pounded on the wood shutters. They didn't budge.

We were prisoners in the old home . . . trapped, with no way out.

28

We tried all of the windows, pounding on the shutters, trying to open them, but it was no use. Even though the shutters were old, they wouldn't break. I tried to open the door again. No luck. The three of us tried to break it down, throwing all of our weight against it. Even *that* didn't work.

And all the while, we could hear the horrible laughter of the woman just beyond the house and the yipping and yapping of coyotes.

I looked for another way out, but there wasn't

any. There wasn't a basement, and I scanned the ceiling to see if there was an attic door. I found nothing. There was nowhere to go.

The three of us stood in the middle of the room, scared out of our minds. If you've ever been trapped in a room like we were, you know how it feels.

The woman's voice and the yipping coyotes began to fade. They sounded like they were moving away. Soon, we could no longer hear them. In fact, we didn't hear anything. No crickets, no birds, nothing. The silence was eerie.

"What's going on?" Haleigh whispered.

I shook my head. *"I don't know,"* I whispered back.

"How are we going to get out of here?" Brent asked.

Haleigh walked to the door and tried it again. It didn't move an inch.

"Something really bizarre is going on," I said.

"No kidding?" Brent said, with more than a hint of sarcasm. "I would have never known."

"There's got to be a way out of here," Haleigh said. She went around the room, pushing the shutters, but it was no use. They wouldn't open, and they wouldn't break.

"It's like the house doesn't want us to leave," I said.

"Somebody—or some*thing*—doesn't want us to leave, that's for sure," Haleigh said. She gave up trying to break the shutters, and the three of us stood in the middle of the room. I hadn't noticed it before, but my entire body was trembling with fear.

"And nobody knows we're here," Brent said in despair. "No one knows where to come looking for us. My mom and dad are—"

Brent was interrupted by a creaking sound. We turned.

The front door was slowly opening!

That alone was horrifying enough, but one thing I noticed right away was the fact that light from outside wasn't pouring in. Outside, it appeared murky and dark, like night had fallen. Even the inside of the house seemed darker.

But we've only been in here for a few minutes, I thought. *It's the middle of the day! How did it get dark so fast?*

Then, as the door opened wider, it was clear that it wasn't opening on its own, because we could see the dark silhouette of a woman and two coyotes standing in the doorway!

29

If I had been frightened before, it was nothing like the fear I was now feeling. Before, I had been scared. Now, I was completely horrified. What was going on wasn't real. It *couldn't* be real.

And yet, I was seeing it, experiencing every terrifying detail. The front door had opened to a dark, gloomy day. Standing in the doorway was the silhouette of a woman and two coyotes! I recognized her face from her picture in the newspaper! She was wearing a long, gray dress, buttoned up to her neck, and her hair was tied back in a bun.

"Go on," the woman said, speaking to her animals. "Go inside."

The three of us backed against the far wall, as there was nowhere else we could go. I pressed my back hard to the wall, wishing there was some way I could get out of the room, but we were trapped.

The two coyotes sauntered into the room, followed by the woman.

"Good boys," she said to the animals, and she paid no attention to us. It was as if we weren't even there.

And maybe we aren't, I thought. *Or maybe the woman and the two coyotes aren't. Maybe we're dreaming.*

The woman turned and seemed to look right at us. It was a horrifying moment, but she acted as if she hadn't seen us.

That's because she can't, I thought. *Somehow, we are stuck in some space or time, partway between her world and ours.*

Is that how dreams work? I used to think dreams were fun, because of all the crazy things that happened. Of course, when a monster is chasing you or something else scary is happening, it's not fun at all. But I remembered how cool it had been when I was dreaming about flying. I'd actually been able to control what I was dreaming about.

"Guys," I said quietly. *"She doesn't even know we're here. In her world, she can't see us."*

"That doesn't make any sense," said Haleigh.

"Yeah," Brent whispered. *"How is it that we can see her, but she can't see us?"*

The woman walked into the bedroom, and the two coyotes followed.

"Let's get out of here while we can!" Haleigh hissed, and she sprang for the door.

"Haleigh, wait!" I whispered. *"I think that—"*

But it was too late. Haleigh was already out the door, and Brent was right behind her. They raced outside . . . and immediately vanished into thin air!

30

I ran to the door, forgetting all about the woman and the coyotes in the bedroom. I stopped when I reached the doorway, suddenly shocked by the surroundings I was seeing.

The world beyond the doorway had changed. Only moments before, it had been dark and gray. Now, however, the gloom had been replaced by a hazy, blue mist. Everything was dull and fuzzy, out of focus, like I was seeing things through a blurry glass lens. I rubbed my eyes, but the gauzy vision remained.

Suddenly, I saw Haleigh and Brent. They were backed against a tree near the house, surrounded by coyotes. There were six of the animals, swirling around, teeth bared, threatening. Although they remained a few feet away from my friends, there was no telling what the vicious creatures would do next.

And their *eyes*.

The coyotes' eyes were glowing bright red. They flashed and winked as the animals ran around the tree, preventing Haleigh and Brent from running away.

"How did you get in here?" a voice said.

Stunned, I turned to see the woman. She was looking at me, and she looked just as surprised to see me as I was to see her! Even the two coyotes were looking at me. They had curious expressions on their faces. They seemed surprised, too.

"You . . . you can see me?" I stammered.

"Of course," the woman said. "But how did you get in here? You weren't there a moment ago."

I'm dreaming again, I thought. *Or, somehow, my mind is creating this scene. My mind is imagining everything.*

Outside, Brent and Haleigh were backed against the tree, terrified. The coyotes continued to circle them, as wild and vicious as ever.

I stared at them.

Go away, I thought, as I looked at the pack of animals. *Go away, right now. Leave Brent and Haleigh alone.*

Incredibly, the coyotes suddenly vanished! One second they were there, and the next, there was no sign of them.

Even Brent and Haleigh couldn't believe it. They stood against the tree, looking around, wondering what had happened to the animals.

"How did you get here?" the woman asked again.

"I'm not sure," I said. "But I think I'm dreaming."

"Well, I'm not dreaming," the woman said.

She watched me cautiously, like I might pose a threat to her.

"Tell me," I said, "what year is it?"

She looked puzzled. "Why, it's 1917," she said.

1917! I thought. *Not only am I dreaming, but I'm dreaming back in time!*

I thought carefully. "Are you the woman who made the curse? About the coyotes?"

Her jaw suddenly went slack, and her mouth hung open. "How did you know about that?" she demanded. "I haven't told anyone."

I shook my head. "I don't know how I know," I said. "But I do. I don't have any idea what's going on, but I know that if you put a curse on the town, it's going to happen."

"Nonsense," the woman said. "I'm not a witch. But nobody believes me because they think I talk to coyotes. They think I cast a spell on the weather and even caused people to become sick. Ridiculous."

She reached down and scratched one of the coyotes behind his ears, and the animal wagged his tail happily, just like a dog.

"I don't think you're a witch," I said. "But I'm from the future, and I know that if you place a curse on the town, years from now, coyotes with red eyes are going to begin to appear. I don't know what will happen, but I know it won't be good."

Brent and Haleigh appeared in the doorway. They glanced nervously at the woman and her coyotes.

"The coyotes surrounding us disappeared!" Brent said.

I turned. "I know," I said. "I made them."

"This just gets weirder and weirder," Haleigh said.

"Who are you talking to?" the woman asked.

I turned to face her. "You can't see my friends?" I asked.

She shook her head. "No," she replied.

Erica, I thought, *you are freaking out. You have gone totally crazy.*

I turned back around and looked at Brent and Haleigh. "Can you see the woman and the coyotes standing there?" I asked.

Brent and Haleigh nodded.

"She says she can't see you," I said. "But I can see her and hear her. I can talk to her. She says that this is the year 1917."

"No way," Brent said.

"That's what she says," I said with a nod.

The woman spoke. "Who are you talking to?" she asked again.

"I know this is going to sound really weird," I replied, "but, somehow, I think we've traveled back in time within one of my dreams. It's funny, though. I didn't think I was sleeping."

"You have strange clothing," the woman said,

153

looking me up and down. I was wearing blue jeans and a T-shirt . . . clothing she wasn't familiar with.

"That's because I'm from the future," I said. "And I know all of this is really weird, but please don't put a curse on the coyotes or the town. If you do, it will really happen."

"I'm not a witch," the woman insisted again. "But everyone thinks I am. They won't leave me alone. Especially that newspaper reporter. He's the one spreading lies about me."

"Maybe I can talk to him," I said. "Maybe he just doesn't understand."

And, at that very moment, a figure appeared behind Brent and Haleigh. He was tall and thin and dressed in a black suit. He was carrying a large, old-fashioned camera with a very large flash bulb attached. It looked nothing at all like the digital cameras of the future. The man's eyes burned with anger, his mouth was closed tightly, and I knew right away that I was about to come face to face with the newspaper reporter . . . whether I wanted to or not!

31

"It's time for you to leave this town," the newspaper reporter snarled. His voice was deep and husky. He meant business.

"But she's not a witch!" I protested.

"Yes, she is!" the man replied. "Last year, she put a curse on the weather, and we had no rain. All of our crops dried up."

"I did no such thing!" the woman insisted.

The two coyotes had been standing at the woman's side, silent and motionless. Now, however, they appeared agitated. The hackles on their backs stiffened, and they began growling softly.

"See?!?!" the newspaper reporter said. "This woman makes friends with wild animals. She must be a witch!"

I didn't know what I could do or say to make the man believe that the woman wasn't a witch.

"Leave my house!" the woman ordered. "Leave, and never come back!"

"I'm not leaving until you leave town," the man said angrily. "Nobody wants you here."

"That's because you told them I was a witch," the woman said.

"And I'm going to keep writing about you in the newspaper until you are forced to leave," the reporter snarled. Then, he raised his camera and snapped a photo. There was an explosion of white light as the flash bulb went off.

But the brightness never faded. Normally, a camera flash is bright for a split second, and then it's gone. Now, however, the whiteness seemed to hang in the air. It was very strange. Light hung in the room like a strange, mysterious cloud.

The woman, too, saw the strange light, and she

began looking around. The newspaper reporter took a step back. His eyes were filled with fear.

"You're doing this!" he cried. He was still angry, but now there was a hint of fear in his voice. "See?!?! I told you! I told you she was a witch!"

The reporter spun and ran off, swinging his large camera at his side.

The room grew brighter and brighter, but I couldn't see where the light was coming from.

Haleigh and Brent began to fade, as if the light was making them vanish. The woman and her two coyotes also became muddled in the light. Soon, it was so bright that I had to shield my eyes. The light was actually painful, and it was then that I realized something.

We had been wrong.

About the woman.

She was doing this. She was a witch, and she was causing the light.

I closed my eyes, but the light was still there, pressing against my head, squeezing tighter and tighter. I grew dizzy, and I fell to the floor, onto my back. The white light pressed down upon me. I felt light-headed. I could hear sounds around me, like the coyotes scratching their nails on the wood floor. And the witch was speaking, muttering something, calling my name.

"It's too late, Erica. Much too late, Erica. Erica. Erica. Erica . . . ."

32

". . . *Erica. Erica. Can you hear me, Erica?*"

"D . . . don't . . . don't," I stammered. My voice was barely a whisper.

"Erica, this is Doctor Winslow speaking. Can you hear me?"

My thoughts were muddled, and the bright white light gnawed painfully at my head.

"Light," I said. "Hurts."

"It will go away. You've had a bad accident.

You're in the hospital."

Accident? I thought. *Doctor Winslow? Hospital? What's going on?*

Gradually, I began to make out darker shapes, but everything was still fuzzy. I blinked a few times, and that helped to clear things up. Something moved above me. The form was fuzzy and out of focus, but I realized it was Dr. Winslow. She's been my doctor since I was little.

"How are you feeling?" she asked.

I blinked a few more times, and her face came into focus. She had dark hair and was wearing a light blue laboratory coat. A stethoscope hung from her neck.

"My head hurts," I said.

"I'm sure it does," she said. "You had quite a fall."

"I'm thirsty, too," I said.

Doctor Winslow helped me sit up. Then, she drew a glass of water from a nearby sink and helped me sip.

I looked around. In the doorway, a nurse appeared, along with Mom and Cole, and they stopped at my bed.

"How are you feeling?" Mom asked, repeating the doctor's question. She sounded worried.

"Okay, I guess, except for my head," I replied.

"You're lucky you weren't hurt worse than you are," Mom said. "You have a concussion."

"What's that?" I asked. It seemed to me I'd heard the word before, but I wasn't sure what it meant.

"It means you've hit your head very hard," Doctor Winslow explained. "You'll be okay, but your head is going to hurt for a while, and I'd like to keep you here overnight, so we can keep an eye on you. Concussions are serious."

"You're lucky Cole found you in the garage," Mom said.

"We hadda call the 'bambalance," Cole said.

"Ambulance," Mom corrected. Then, she spoke to me. "You were climbing the shelves when you fell and hit your head on the concrete floor."

My memory began coming back to me: going into the garage, climbing the shelves, and falling backward.

But I got up, I thought. *I was okay. I hit my head, and I remember it hurting, but I got up, picked up the mess, and left. I wasn't hurt that bad.*

Was I?

Apparently, I had been hurt worse than I thought.

"What about the coyotes?" I asked. "And the lady in her house?"

Mom looked at me, puzzled. "What coyotes? What lady?"

"Brent and Haleigh and I went to an old house where a woman used to live. We traveled back in time and . . . ."

I began to realize how silly it all sounded.

None of that ever happened, I thought. *It all must have happened in my mind, while I was unconscious.*

As if reading my thoughts, Doctor Winslow spoke. "Your mind can play tricks on you in times like these," she said. "You've been at the hospital for a couple of hours, ever since the ambulance brought you in."

"But . . . but Brent and Haleigh," I stammered. "And Miss Levine. The library. The old house. The newspaper reporter . . . ."

It was such a strange feeling, to think all of those things had happened . . . only to realize that it was all just my own imagination, a very vivid dream.

Dreams within dreams, even.

But if I thought things were strange then, they were about to get a *lot* stranger—beginning with a visit from Haleigh and Brent later that evening.

33

Mom and Cole stayed with me for a little while after Doctor Winslow left. After they left, I fell asleep and awoke when Dad came in to see me. I thought he was going to be mad at me for climbing on the shelves, but he wasn't. He didn't give me a lecture or anything.

"I think you've learned your lesson," was all he said.

I nodded. "I won't be climbing on shelves any more," I said.

After Dad left, a nurse came in with a tray of

food. It was lousy and tasted worse than the meals at school. There was a piece of meat that was supposed to be chicken, but it tasted like cardboard. I ate only one bite. The slice of bread was soggy, and I didn't eat it at all. But there was a banana, and it was pretty good. And the glass of milk was cold and refreshing.

A television hung on the wall, and the remote sat on a small table next to my bed. I surfed through the channels until I found a game show.

"Surprise," a voice said, and Haleigh and Brent appeared in the doorway.

"Hi, guys!" I said. I was happy to see them, and I picked up the remote control and turned off the television.

"We heard about your accident," Brent said. "My mom said she saw the ambulance at your house this morning. Everyone was freaked out."

"You were lucky," Haleigh said. "Does your head still hurt?"

I nodded. "Yeah," I replied. "But Doctor Winslow says I'm going to be all right. I have to stay the night here in the hospital, but she says I can probably go home tomorrow. I have a concussion, but she says I'm going to be okay."

Brent approached my bed and leaned over.

"You've sure got a big bump," he said. "Did you get knocked out?"

I nodded again. "Yeah," I said. "And while I was unconscious, I had the freakiest experience."

"So did we," Haleigh said, and she walked to my bed and stood next to Brent. "Last night, I saw two coyotes with glowing red eyes."

"So did I," Brent said.

"You did?" I gasped. I was shocked. I hadn't told Haleigh or Brent about the coyotes, because the entire episode had happened in my mind. Everything that happened from the moment I fell and hit my head hadn't been real.

"Yeah," Haleigh said. "There's a curse on the town from a long time ago. We found out about it at the library."

What? I thought. *That's what happened while I was knocked out! We found out about the lady and her curse when we went to the library!*

I wanted to tell Brent and Haleigh about my dream, about what happened while I was unconscious, but I decided to wait until they told me their story.

"We went there to see if we could find anything

out," Brent explained. "While we were there, we talked with Miss Levine. She told us that when she was a kid, they'd heard about the curse, and she and her friends used to scare each other with their own stories."

Just like in my dream! I thought.

"Yeah," Haleigh continued. "She said that years ago, a woman was accused of being a witch—"

"—But she wasn't," I interjected.

Brent and Haleigh looked at each other.

"How did you know?" Brent asked.

"I'm not sure," I said. "But keep going."

"Anyway," Haleigh continued, "Miss Levine says that, years ago, it was in the newspapers and everything."

"In 1917," I said.

Brent and Haleigh were shocked, and both of their mouths hung open in silent disbelief.

"How . . . how did you know?" Haleigh whispered.

"I'm not sure," I said. "But I do. I think that somehow, when I was knocked out, I went back in time in a dream. You guys were with me. We went to the lady's house. I talked to her."

"What did you say to her?" Brent asked.

168

"I told her not to put a curse on the town," I said. "I told her that if she did, it would really work, and red-eyed coyotes would come to the city in the future. I met the newspaper reporter, too. What else did you guys find out?"

"Miss Levine says there are a lot of old newspaper articles about the woman," Haleigh said. "She's going to gather some of them and have them ready for us by tomorrow."

I remembered how, while I was unconscious, I went to Haleigh's house, where she had a bunch of copied newspaper clippings from a long time ago. I remembered what they'd said, about the woman who was believed to be a witch because she had befriended two coyotes. And how we had walked to the library and spoke with Miss Levine. In the few hours that I had been unconscious, it seemed like a few days had passed.

But that was all in my head, I thought. *That was all just my imagination.*

Was it?

How could I have been unconscious and have all those crazy things happen? Even now it seemed so real, so clear in my mind, and I didn't understand how my brain could do something like that.

I'd have my answer the following day, when we would discover that the truth was even more shocking and more mysterious than anything we could have ever thought possible.

34

That night, I slept all the way through without dreaming. I had been worried, because I thought I might have yet another nightmare about vicious, red-eyed coyotes. I was relieved to awaken in the morning to sunshine streaming through the window and a bustle of activity in the hospital. My head still hurt a little bit, but not as bad as the day before.

After breakfast, Doctor Winslow came in and looked me over. She said that I was okay, that I could go home. Mom and Cole came to the hospital shortly after that. Doctor Winslow and Mom talked for a moment while Cole bounced on my bed. He was being his normal, pesky self, but I didn't mind.

The bad news was that I wasn't allowed to go to the library. On the way home, Mom said that Doctor Winslow had told her that I was to stay in bed for the rest of the day, just in case. She said I could have a dizzy spell, faint, and fall again . . . and maybe hurt myself even worse.

Bummer. I was really hoping to go to the library with Haleigh and Brent.

However, that wasn't a problem. When I spoke to Haleigh on the phone later that morning and told her I couldn't leave my bed, she said that she and Brent would go to the library, make copies of whatever Miss Levine found, and bring them to me to read.

Later that afternoon, the doorbell rang.

"I get it! I get it!" Cole shouted, and I heard his feet pattering through the living room as he raced to the front door. Then, I could hear Brent's and Haleigh's voices. The front door closed, and in seconds, my two friends were standing in my bedroom doorway. Haleigh had a thick folder containing papers tucked beneath her arm.

"How are you feeling?" Brent asked.

"Fine," I said. "My head hurts a little. But I'm glad you came. I'm bored to death."

"You won't be for long," Haleigh said, and she came into my bedroom, followed by Brent.

"What did you find out?" I asked.

Haleigh and Brent looked at each other.

"We're not sure," Brent said. "We don't know what to think of it."

Haleigh opened the folder and pulled out a few pieces of paper. They were copies of old newspaper clippings.

"There's a lot here," Haleigh said, "and you don't have to read them all. But there is one story that you are really going to want to see."

She flipped through the pages, located the one she was looking for, and pulled it out. Then, she sat on my bed.

"We found out that the stories about the woman were true," she said. "There are a few stories about how the woman was accused of being a witch. She insisted that she wasn't, but most people in town didn't believe her.

"Finally, she got mad and decided to tell

everyone that she was a witch and that she was going to place a curse on the town."

"The coyotes?" I asked.

Haleigh nodded. "Yep," she replied.

"But she never did," Brent said.

"She never did what?" I asked.

"She never placed a curse on the town," Haleigh answered. "You see, a mysterious girl came to her home one day. While she was there, the newspaper reporter showed up. There was some sort of argument, and the reporter ran off. No one knew what the girl said to the woman, but she never threatened the town with a curse. After that, the people left her alone, and there were no more stories in the paper about the woman or any coyotes."

"I don't get it," I said.

"Maybe you will when you see this," Haleigh said. She handed the sheet of paper to me, and I looked at it. It was a copy of an old newspaper article from 1917. Beneath the story was a grainy picture of the woman standing next to a young girl.

And the girl in the photo was me!

35

I stared at the old news clipping. The black and white photo was grainy and a little blurry, but it sure looked like me.

I read the article. It was strange, reading about something I had done nearly one hundred years ago! In the story, no one knew who the girl was, where she came from, or where she went.

"That's more than crazy!" Brent said. "That picture was taken before you were born!"

"Anything is possible when you dream," I said. "And somehow, when I was unconscious, I was able to go back in time and change history."

"I wonder if you could do that again," Haleigh said. "Think about it: if you could go back in time when you dream, you could change things!"

I shook my head. "I don't think that's such a good idea," I replied. "Maybe this time it was, to stop the woman and the curse. But changing history might get us into a lot of trouble."

"I guess you're right," Haleigh said.

Still, I wondered. I wondered if I would be able to do something like that again. I wondered if I could travel around in my dreams, back in time.

But as the days and weeks passed, it became more and more unlikely that I could. The strange episode had occurred only because I'd hit my head. Sure, that didn't explain how or why it happened, but as the nights passed, I realized that I wouldn't be able to do it again.

I told my parents what had happened while I was out cold, how I had traveled back in time. I even showed them the picture to prove it.

"The girl in the picture looks a little like you," Mom said. "But that picture is from 1917. There's no way it could be you."

I tried to tell her that it really did happen, but she said it wasn't possible. She said the entire experience was because of my head injury. Finally, I gave up trying to convince her.

And I never saw any more coyotes with glowing red eyes. Still, the fact remained that, years ago, the woman had actually placed some sort of curse on the coyotes, and it had worked. I knew this because I saw the coyotes before I had my accident. Brent and Haleigh saw them, too. But while I was unconscious, I had gone back in time and changed things.

But if I went back in time and changed the future, why did we see the coyotes at all? I had no answer.

November came. The air turned cold and crisp. The leaves changed from green to shades of red, copper, yellow, and orange. Soon, the colorful fall leaves would turn brown and be torn from their branches by the autumn winds. Snow would fall. Usually, we don't get a lot of snow, but I was hoping that this year, we'd get a ton. I love building snowmen and snow forts and having snowball fights with my friends.

Then, one day at school, Haleigh, Brent, and I sat in the lunchroom, talking about my accident and my strange dream and how I had been able to travel back in time. We must have been talking a little too loud, because a kid at the table behind us came over and sat down near us.

"I didn't mean to eavesdrop," he said, "but I heard you talking about your dreams and how you went back in time."

I looked at Brent and Haleigh.

"Do we know you?" Haleigh asked. She didn't intend to be mean, but that's the way it sounded.

The boy shook his head. "No," he said. "My family just moved here from Oregon. Did that really happen? Did you really travel back in time during a dream, after you fell and hit your head?"

I nodded. "I know it sounds bizarre," I replied, "but it's true. Every word of it."

His name was Jacob Brenner, and he was really interested in hearing all about my dreams and how I'd gone back in time and actually changed the future.

"That would be cool," he said, "but the best adventures aren't dreams. The best adventures are real, like what we did last summer."

"What was that?" Brent asked.

"I'm an oceanaut," he replied.

"An oceanaut?" I asked. "What's an oceanaut?"

"It's a technical name for a scuba diver," Jacob said. "Last summer, my sister and I dove to a sunken submarine to save the ocean from being poisoned."

I gasped. "I saw that on the news!" I said. "That was *you?!?!*"

Jacob nodded proudly. "That was me and my sister," he said. "It was dangerous."

"I saw that on television, too," Haleigh said.

Jacob shook his head. "Then, you only got part of the story. What really happened was *scary.*"

"Tell us about it!" I said.

"Okay," Jacob replied. He took a sip of milk and began his incredible, horrifying story of being an oceanaut off the coast of Oregon . . . .

Next:

America's #1 Series for MAXIMUM Chills!

#29: Oregon Oceanauts

Continue on for a FREE preview!

1

As I gazed out over the choppy sea, emotions swept over me like the waves churning before my eyes. I was nervous, and I'm not a bit ashamed to admit I was a little afraid. After all: what we were about to do was risky and dangerous.

But it had to be done. We had to succeed. If we didn't, the ocean would face a terrible environmental disaster.

There were two of us that would play an important role in the mission: me and my younger

183

sister, Shannon. She was seated next to me on the boat as it bobbed up and down in the sea. Above, the sun glowed like a lemon drop in the blue sky. Below, glittering diamonds reflected off the choppy seas. The only sounds were the wind in my ears and the water lapping at the side of the *Sea Falcon,* the big research boat we were on. Several other vessels were moored nearby.

"How long, Jacob?" Shannon asked.

"I don't know," I replied. "But I'm sure we'll be suiting up soon."

On the deck in front of us, our gear lay in two piles: wetsuits, vests, and air tanks. We didn't want to suit up until we were ready to dive, as being in a wetsuit in the hot sun would cause us to bake. We were waiting for word from the mission specialists that the dive was a go.

Finally, one of the scientists came up from below and told us it was time. We suited up in silence with the help of two laboratory technicians. They were very professional and knew what they were doing. And they treated us like adults, not kids. I liked that. What we were doing was important, and if it could have been done by adults, it would have.

But it couldn't. This mission needed small people—kids—to perform the dangerous tasks at the bottom of the ocean. Sound crazy? That's what I thought . . . at first.

After we'd donned our wetsuits, checked our air tanks, and performed other necessary tests, we were ready.

And I really thought we would succeed. I thought we would be heroes.

But as Shannon and I slipped backward off the boat and into the crystal blue water, I had no idea of the horrors waiting for us in the murky depths of the Pacific Ocean.

2

For you to understand what's going on, I need to go back to where everything began. On May ninth of this year, I was a pretty typical kid leading a pretty typical life. I went to school, did my homework (most of the time), played pranks on my sister, and played basketball with my friends.

But that night, I saw something that was soon to change my life and lead to a series of adventures most kids my age don't get to have.

My sister, my mom, and I live in Portland, a city

in the very northern region of Oregon, which borders Washington. In fact, we live so close to Washington that I can ride my bicycle there. Not many other kids in the country could say they do that.

Where we live is really cool. Portland is the biggest city in the state. Summers are great; it's sunny and warm. In the winter, we get a lot of rain, but hardly any snow, because it doesn't stay cold long enough. And Portland is the home of the Portland Trail Blazers, my favorite basketball team. That used to be my favorite sport—basketball. But not anymore. You see, I've since discovered a new sport. A sport I love more than basketball or any other sport: scuba diving.

I'd already known what scuba diving was, as I'd seen shows on television showing men and women dressed in wetsuits and special gear, staying under water for long periods of time, breathing air through a mouthpiece called a regulator that connected to hose that was affixed to a tank on their backs. I thought it was pretty cool, but I never imagined myself ever doing anything like that. After all: I was just a kid, and I'd never seen kids scuba diving on television before . . . until May ninth.

I was surfing through the channels on TV when

my sister, Shannon, came into the room. Shannon is eleven—one year younger than me. We get along pretty well, but I play pranks on her sometimes and she gets mad at me. Once, I put a plastic spider under the covers in her bed. When she found it later that night, she totally freaked out. She thought it was real and screamed her head off. Mom ran into the room, worried. And I got in trouble! I was grounded for a week and couldn't go out of the house, except for when I went to school.

"What are you watching?" Shannon said as she sat on the other end of the couch.

"Nothing yet," I replied.

I scanned the channels, searching for something fun to watch.

Finally, something interesting appeared on the screen: a man scuba diving. All around him, a school of fish hung in the blue-green water, swirling like colorful clouds. The fish weren't scared of him at all. They swarmed around him, more curious than frightened. It was mesmerizing to watch the man move in slow motion in the water, with shiny bubbles of air emerging from his mouthpiece and rising to the surface.

"Hey, that's cool," Shannon said. "Leave it on that channel."

I put the remote on the armrest and sat back to watch. The scuba diver hung in the water, motionless, watching fish of all sizes swirl around him.

"I'd like to do that," Shannon said.

Me, too, I thought. But I knew it would never happen. You see, I'm very small for my age. Shannon is, too. When I play basketball, I'm not very good at shooting or getting rebounds, because I'm so short. But I have one great advantage: because I'm small, I can move very, very fast . . . much faster than anyone else in my grade. When I play basketball with my friends, everyone wants me on their team because I'm so quick. I'm also pretty good at dodgeball, soccer, and other sports where you have to move fast.

But I was certain that when it came to scuba diving, I would never be able to do it until I got bigger. I figured the air tank alone probably weighed more than I did, and I'd never be able to carry it on my back. Plus, I didn't have a lot of money. I was sure that scuba diving would cost more than what I had in my piggy bank.

It will be years before I'll be able to take a course

and learn to scuba dive, I thought. *I will probably—*

And that's when my thought was interrupted by a horrific sound of crashing metal and breaking glass on the street in front of our house.

3

Shannon and I leapt from the couch and turned, looking out the big window facing our front yard. In the street, two cars had collided, and both front ends were a mangled mess. The vehicle on the left was a white car. Its hood was crinkled like an accordion, and gray smoke boiled up from the engine.

The other vehicle was a van. The front of it was smashed in, and the windshield had shattered. Tiny particles of glass were sprinkled on the road.

"Call nine-one-one!" I shouted to Shannon. She

raced to grab the phone while I ran out of the living room, through the front door, and across the yard.

What if someone is hurt? I wondered. My thoughts were frantic, my mind anxious. *If someone is hurt bad, I don't know what to do.*

Thankfully, a woman was getting out of the white car. It appeared she was the only one inside, and it didn't seem like she was hurt.

But the man in the van had a bloody nose. As he opened the door, I could see that the vehicle's air bag had deployed. Now it was deflated, and it crumpled over the hood like a battered circus balloon.

"Are you all right?" I asked as I approached. Which was kind of a silly question, being that I could see blood running from his nose, over his mouth, and onto his chin.

"I think I'm fine," the man said, "except for this." And with that, he placed his thumb and finger to his nose, closing his nostrils to stem the flow of blood. "When the air bag went off, it knocked my fist into my face. I gave myself a bloody nose."

"I'll get you a towel!" I said, and I spun and ran into the house. In the living room, Shannon was on the phone talking to the emergency operator, giving the person details about the accident. I ran past her, turned, and went down the hall and into the bathroom.

A cold, wet towel, I thought. *That would probably help.*

Without thinking, I grabbed one of Mom's good towels—the ones we aren't supposed to use—that were hanging from the rack. She says they match the curtains, and they're only for decoration . . . which is kind of silly, if you ask me. After all: what good is a towel hanging on the rack if you can't use it?

I ran the cold water for a moment, then soaked the towel and wrung it out. I ran down the hall and through the living room, where Shannon had just ended her phone call.

"The lady said she was sending someone right away," she said. "Is that guy hurt bad?"

"I think it's just a bloody nose," I said as I darted out the front door. Shannon followed as I sprinted across the lawn.

The woman that had been driving the white car was near the curb, talking on a small phone. The man was sitting on the sidewalk, still holding his nose, when I approached. Other neighbors, alerted by the crash, were coming out of their houses.

"Here," I said to the man, and I held out the cold, wet towel.

"Thanks," he said. He balled the towel around his nose and tipped his head back. "I haven't had a bloody nose in years," he said. "Once, I fell forward in a boat and couldn't catch myself. Smacked myself a good one and broke my nose."

In the distance, I heard a siren.

"Help is coming," Shannon said. "I just called nine-one-one."

"Thank you," the man said, still holding his head back. "I think I'm going to be okay. Looks like we were both lucky this time."

He was right. As it turned out, the woman's car had a broken tie rod. While I don't really know what that is, my mom later told me it controls the car's steering. When the tie rod broke, the woman lost control and swerved into the man's oncoming van.

I thought Mom was going to be mad at me for using one of her good towels, but she wasn't. She said she was glad we acted fast and did the right thing. Mom said she was proud of both Shannon and me, saying we'd done the right things when it really mattered.

I didn't really think I'd done anything that important. I mean, all I did was get a towel for the guy. Shannon called nine-one-one. Nobody was hurt badly, and neither the woman nor the man had to be taken to the hospital. Two wreckers came, cleaned the street, and hauled away the two crippled vehicles. Mom took us out for pizza and ice cream, and we went home.

A week later, I'd forgotten all about the accident . . . until a letter addressed to Shannon and me came in the mail one afternoon.

4

I had been playing basketball with my friends at the park. The day was sunny and hot, and around five o'clock, our teams broke up. Most of us had to go home to get cleaned up and ready for dinner.

When I walked into the house, Mom was on the phone. She held her finger to her lips, indicating I should be silent.

"Yes," she was saying, "that's right. And if you—"

I didn't pay any more attention to what she was

saying, because Mom picked up a letter that was on the couch, smiled, and handed it to me while she talked on the phone.

I took the letter. It was addressed to me and Shannon. In the upper-left hand corner, there was a small cartoon character—a scuba diver. Beneath it were the words *Waters of Wonder Scuba Shop.*

I frowned. *Why would Shannon and I get a letter from a scuba shop?*

Strange.

I opened the letter, not sure what to expect. It contained a handwritten letter in blue ink. I unfolded the paper and read.

Dear Jacob and Shannon:

I contacted the police department to get your names and address so I could send a letter of thanks. Last week, I was involved in a car crash on your street. You two helped out by bringing me a towel and contacting the authorities.

Although my injury was minor, I deeply appreciate both of you coming to my assistance, and I would like to repay you. I am the owner of Waters of Wonder Scuba Shop, and I would like to offer both of you free scuba diving lessons. The course begins next week and lasts for one month. Classes will be held in the classroom and the pool at my shop, and your final test for certification will take place in the ocean.

I was trembling with excitement. I continued to read the letter.

Please let me know at your earliest convenience. There will be others taking the scuba class, and I'll need to reserve the spaces for both of you.

Again, thank you for your help. You might be happy to know that my nose is going to be fine, although it's still a little purple and swollen.

Sincerely,

Morris Lukeman

My mouth hung open as I read the letter over.

Scuba diving class? I thought. *Free? But what about my age? What about my size? Didn't that matter?*

Mr. Lukeman obviously knew how big Shannon and I were.

He must think we're big enough, I thought. *Maybe it doesn't matter how big I am, after all.*

Mom hung up the phone. She saw my surprised expression and smiled.

"Who's the letter from?" she asked.

"The guy we helped last week!" I blurted,

waving the letter in the air. "He wants to give me and Shannon free scuba lessons!"

I gave her the letter to read, just as Shannon strode through the front door.

"Shannon!" I said. "You're not going to believe this, but that guy says we can take scuba lessons for free!"

"What guy?" Shannon said.

"The guy in the car accident last week! He owns a scuba diving shop, and he wants to thank us by giving us free scuba diving lessons!"

"That's awesome!" Shannon exclaimed.

"This is very nice of him," Mom said when she'd finished reading the letter.

"Let me see," Shannon said, and she held out her hand and took the letter from Mom.

"Can we?" I asked.

Mom shrugged. "I don't see why not," she said. "It sounds like a fun adventure for the both of you."

Oh, it would be an adventure, all right.

An adventure . . . into disaster.

ABOUT THE AUTHOR

Johnathan Rand is the author of more than 65 books, with well over 4 million copies in print. Series include **AMERICAN CHILLERS, MICHIGAN CHILLERS, FREDDIE FERNORTNER, FEARLESS FIRST GRADER**, and **THE ADVENTURE CLUB.** He's also co-authored a novel for teens (with Christopher Knight) entitled **PANDEMIA**. When not traveling, Rand lives in northern Michigan with his wife and three dogs. He is also the only author in the world to have a store that sells only his works: **CHILLERMANIA!** is located in Indian River, Michigan. Johnathan Rand is not always at the store, but he has been known to drop by frequently. Find out more at:

www.americanchillers.com

JOIN THE FREE AMERICAN CHILLERS FAN CLUB!

It's easy to join . . . and best of all, it's FREE!
Find out more today by visiting:

WWW.AMERICANCHILLERS.COM

And don't forget to browse the on-line
superstore, where you can order books, hats,
shirts, and lots more cool stuff!

Johnathan Rand travels internationally for school visits and book signings! For booking information, call:

1 (231) 238-0338!

www.americanchillers.com

Other books by Johnathan Rand:

Michigan Chillers:

#1: Mayhem on Mackinac Island
#2: Terror Stalks Traverse City
#3: Poltergeists of Petoskey
#4: Aliens Attack Alpena
#5: Gargoyles of Gaylord
#6: Strange Spirits of St. Ignace
#7: Kreepy Klowns of Kalamazoo
#8: Dinosaurs Destroy Detroit
#9: Sinister Spiders of Saginaw
#10: Mackinaw City Mummies
#11: Great Lakes Ghost Ship
#12: AuSable Alligators
#13: Gruesome Ghouls of Grand Rapids
#14: Bionic Bats of Bay City

American Chillers:

#1: The Michigan Mega-Monsters
#2: Ogres of Ohio
#3: Florida Fog Phantoms
#4: New York Ninjas
#5: Terrible Tractors of Texas
#6: Invisible Iguanas of Illinois
#7: Wisconsin Werewolves
#8: Minnesota Mall Mannequins
#9: Iron Insects Invade Indiana
#10: Missouri Madhouse
#11: Poisonous Pythons Paralyze Pennsylvania
#12: Dangerous Dolls of Delaware
#13: Virtual Vampires of Vermont
#14: Creepy Condors of California
#15: Nebraska Nightcrawlers
#16: Alien Androids Assault Arizona
#17: South Carolina Sea Creatures
#18: Washington Wax Museum
#19: North Dakota Night Dragons
#20: Mutant Mammoths of Montana
#21: Terrifying Toys of Tennessee
#22: Nuclear Jellyfish of New Jersey
#23: Wicked Velociraptors of West Virginia
#24: Haunting in New Hampshire
#25: Mississippi Megalodon
#26: Oklahoma Outbreak
#27: Kentucky Komodo Dragons
#28: Curse of the Connecticut Coyotes

Freddie Fernortner, Fearless First Grader:

#1: The Fantastic Flying Bicycle
#2: The Super-Scary Night Thingy
#3: A Haunting We Will Go
#4: Freddie's Dog Walking Service
#5: The Big Box Fort
#6: Mr. Chewy's Big Adventure
#7: The Magical Wading Pool
#8: Chipper's Crazy Carnival
#9: Attack of the Dust Bunnies from Outer Space!
#10: The Pond Monster

Adventure Club series:

#1: Ghost in the Graveyard
#2: Ghost in the Grand
#3: The Haunted Schoolhouse

For Teens:

PANDEMIA: A novel of the bird flu and the end of the world
(written with Christopher Knight)

American Chillers Double Thrillers:

Vampire Nation &
Attack of the Monster Venus Melon

Dont Miss:

**WRITTEN AND READ ALOUD BY JOHNATHAN RAND!
AVAILABLE ONLY ON COMPACT DISC!**

Beware! This special audio CD contains six bone-chilling stories written and read aloud by the master of spooky suspense! American Chillers author Johnathan Rand shares six original tales of terror, including *The People of the Trees, The Mystery of Coyote Lake, Midnight Train, The Phone Call, The House at the End of Gallows Lane,* and the chilling poem, *Dark Night.* Turn out the lights, find a comfortable place, and get ready to enter the strange and bizarre world of **CREEPY CAMPFIRE CHILLERS!**

**ONLY 9.99!
over sixty minutes
of audio!**

**Order online at
www.americanchillers.com
or call toll-free: 1-888-420-4244!**

Also by Johnathan Rand:

GHOST IN THE GRAVEYARD

All AudioCraft books are proudly printed, bound, and manufactured in the United States of America, utilizing American resources, labor, and materials.

USA